Sunny-S

Onoto Watanna

Alpha Editions

This edition published in 2024

ISBN : 9789364735964

Design and Setting By
Alpha Editions
www.alphaedis.com
Email - info@alphaedis.com

As per information held with us this book is in Public Domain.
This book is a reproduction of an important historical work. Alpha Editions uses the best technology to reproduce historical work in the same manner it was first published to preserve its original nature. Any marks or number seen are left intentionally to preserve its true form.

Contents

CHAPTER I .... - 1 -

CHAPTER II .... - 7 -

CHAPTER III .... - 16 -

CHAPTER IV .... - 23 -

CHAPTER V .... - 31 -

CHAPTER VI .... - 41 -

CHAPTER VII .... - 45 -

CHAPTER VIII .... - 53 -

CHAPTER IX .... - 61 -

CHAPTER X .... - 69 -

CHAPTER XI .... - 74 -

CHAPTER XII .... - 80 -

CHAPTER XIII .... - 86 -

CHAPTER XIV .... - 97 -

CHAPTER XV .... - 103 -

CHAPTER XVI .... - 110 -

CHAPTER XVII .... - 119 -

CHAPTER XVIII .... - 127 -

CHAPTER XIX .... - 134 -

CHAPTER XX .... - 139 -

CHAPTER I

Madame Many Smiles was dead. The famous dancer of the House of a Thousand Joys had fluttered out into the Land of Shadows. No longer would poet or reveller vie with each other in doing homage to her whose popularity had known no wane with the years, who had, indeed, become one of the classic objects of art of the city. In a land where one's ancestry is esteemed the all important thing, Madame Many Smiles had stood alone, with neither living relatives nor ancestors to claim her. Who she was, or whence she had come, none knew, but the legend of the House was that on a night of festival she had appeared at the illuminated gates, as a moth, who, beaten by the winds and storms without, seeks shelter in the light and warmth of the joyhouse within.

Hirata had bonded her for a life term. Her remuneration was no more than the geishas' meagre wage, but she was allowed the prerogative of privacy. Her professional duties over, no admiring patron of the gardens might claim her further service. She was free to return to her child, whose cherry blossom skin and fair hair proclaimed clearly the taint of her white blood. Hirata was lenient in his training of the child, for the dancer had brought with her into the House of a Thousand Joys, Daikoku, the God of Fortune, and Hirata could afford to abide the time when the child of the dancer should step into her shoes. But the day had come far ahead of his preparations, and while the dancer was at the zenith of her fame. They were whispering about the gardens that the moth that had fluttered against the House of Joy had fluttered back into the darkness from which she had come. With her she had taken Daikoku.

A profound depression had settled upon the House of a Thousand Joys. Geishas, apprentices and attendants moved aimlessly about their tasks, their smiles mechanical and their motions automatic. The pulse and inspiration of the house had vanished. In the gardens the effect of the news was even more noticeable. Guests were hurriedly departing, turning their cups upside down and calling for their clogs. Tea girls slid in and out on hurried service to the departing guests, and despite the furious orders of the master to affect a gaiety they did not feel, their best efforts were unavailing to dispel the strange veil of gloom that comes ever with death. The star of the House of a Thousand Joys had twinkled out forever.

It was the night of the festival of the Full Moon. The cream of the city were gathered to do honour to the shining Tsuki no Kami in the clear sky above. But the death of the dancer had cast its shadow upon all, and there was a superstitious feeling abroad that it was the omen of a bad year for the city.

In the emptying gardens, Hirata saw impending ruin. Running hither and thither, from house to garden, snapping his fingers, with irritation and fury, he cursed the luck that had befallen him on this night of all nights. The maids shrank before his glance, or silently scurried out of his path. The geishas with automatic smile and quip vainly sought to force a semblance of exhilaration, and the twang of the samisen failed to drown that very low beat of a Buddhist drum in the temple beyond the gardens, where especial honour was to be paid to the famous dancer, who had given her services gratuitously to the temple.

In fury and despair, Hirata turned from the ingratiating women. Again he sought the apartments where the dead dancer lay in state among her robes. Here, with her face at her mother's feet, the child of the dancer prayed unceasingly to the gods that they would permit her to attend her mother upon the long journey to the Meido. Crushed and hurt by a grief that nothing could assuage, only dimly the girl sensed the words of the master, ordering her half peremptorily, half imploringly to prepare for service to the House. Possibly it was his insinuation that for the sake of her mother's honour it behooved her to step into her place, and uphold the fame of the departed one, that aroused her to a mechanical assent. Soon she was in the hands of the dressers, her mourning robes stripped, and the skin tights of the trapese performer substituted.

Hirata, in the gardens, clapping his hands loudly to attract the attention of the departing guests, took his stand upon the little platform. Saluting his patrons with lavish compliments, he begged their indulgence and patience. The light of his House, it was true, so he said, had been temporarily extinguished, but the passing of a dancer meant no more than the falling of a star; and just as there were other stars in the firmament brighter than those that had fallen, so the House of a Thousand Joys possessed in reserve greater beauty and talent than that the guests had generously bestowed their favour upon. The successor to the honourable dancer was bound to please, since she excelled her mother in beauty even as the sun does the moon. He therefore entreated his guests to transfer their gracious patronage to the humble descendant of Madame Many Smiles.

The announcement caused as much of a sensation as the news of the dancer's death had done. There was an element of disapproval and consternation in the glances exchanged in the garden. Nevertheless there was a disposition, governed by curiosity, to at least see the daughter of the famous dancer, who appeared on the night of her mother's death.

A party of American students, with a tutor, were among those still remaining in the gardens. Madame Many Smiles had been an especial favourite with them, their interest possibly due to the fact that she was said to be a half caste. Her beauty and fragility had appealed to them as something especially rare, like a choice piece of cloisonnè, and the romance and mystery that seemed ever about her, captivated their interest, and set them speculating as to what was the true story of this woman, whom the residents pointed to with pride as the masterpiece of their city. An interpreter having translated the words of the manager, there was a general growl of disapproval from the young Americans. However, they, too, remained to see the daughter of Madame Many Smiles, and pushed up near to the rope, along which now came the descendant.

She was a child of possibly fourteen years, her cheeks as vividly red as the poppies in her hair, her long large eyes, with their shining black lashes, strangely bright and feverish. She came tripping across the rope, with a laugh upon her lips, her hair glistening, under the spotlight, almost pure gold in colour. Bobbed and banged in the fashion of the Japanese child, it yet curled about her exquisite young face, and added the last touch of witchery to her beauty. Though her bright red lips were parted in the smile that had made her mother famous, there was something appealing in her wide, blank stare at her audience.

She was dressed in tights, without the customary cape above her, and her graceful, slender limbs were those of extreme youth, supple as elastic from training and ancestry, the lithe, pliable young body of the born trapese performer and dancer. She tossed her parasol to her shoulder, threw up her delicate little pointed chin and laughed across at that sea of faces, throwing right and left her kisses; but the Americans, close to the rope, were observing a phenomenon, for even as her charming little teeth gleamed out in that so captivating smile, a dewdrop appeared to glisten on the child's shining face. Even as she laughed and postured to the music that burst out, there a-tiptoe on the tightrope, the dewdrop fell down her face and disappeared into the sawdust.

Like a flower on the end of a long slender stalk, tossing in the wind, her lovely little head swayed from side to side. Her small, speaking hands, the wrists of which were lovelier than those celebrated by the Japanese poet who for fifteen years had penned his one-line poems to her mother, followed the rhythm of the music, and every part of that delicate young body seemed to sensitively stir and move to the pantomime dance of the tightrope.

In triumph, Hirata heard the loud "Hee-i-i-!" and the sharp indrawing and expulsions of breaths. Scrambling across the room, puffing and expressing his satisfaction, came the Lord of Negato, drunk with sake and amorous for the child upon the rope. He pushed his way past the besieging tea house maidens, who proffered him sweets and tea and sake. His hands went deep into his sleeves, and drew forth a shining bauble. With ingratiating cries to attract her attention, he flung the jewel to the girl upon the rope. Returning his smile, she whirled her fan wide open, caught the gift upon it, and, laughing, tossed it into the air. Juggling and playing with the pretty toy, she kept it twirling in a circle above her, caught it again on her fan, and dropped it down onto the sawdust beneath. Then, like a naughty child, pleased over some trick, she danced back and forth along the rope, as it swung wide with her.

A grunt of anger came from Hirata, who approached near enough for her to see and be intimidated by him, but she kept her gaze well above his head, feigning neither to see him, nor the still pressing Negato. He was calling up to her now, clucking as one might at a dog, and when at last her glance swept his, he threw at her a handful of coin. This also she caught neatly on her opened fan, and then, acting upon a sudden impetuous and impish impulse, she threw right in the face of her besieging admirer. Jumping from the rope to the ground, she smiled and bowed right and left, kissed her hands to her audience, and vanished into the teahouse.

With an imprecation, Hirata followed her into the house. The little maiden, holding the tray, and pausing to solicit the patronage of the Americans, had watched the girl's exit with troubled eyes, and now she said in English:

"*Now* Hirata will beat her."

"What do you mean?" demanded the young man, who had rejected the proffered cup, and was staring at her with such angry eyes that Spring Morning dropped her own, and bobbed her knees in apology for possible offence.

"What do you mean?" repeated Jerry Hammond, determined upon securing an answer, while his friends crowded about interested also in the reply.

Half shielding her face with her fan, the girl replied in a low voice:

"Always the master beats the apprentice who do wrong. When her mother live, he do not touch her child, but now Madame Many Smiles is dead, and Hirata is very angry. He will surely put the lash to-night upon her."

"Do you mean to tell me that that little girl is being beaten because she threw back that dirty gorilla's coin to him?"

Spring Morning nodded, and the tears that came suddenly to her eyes revealed that the girl within had all of her sympathy.

"The devil she is!" Jerry Hammond turned to his friends, "Are we going to stand for this?" demanded Jerry.

"Not by a dashed sight!" shrilly responded the youngest of the party, a youth of seventeen, whose heavy bone-ribbed glasses gave him a preternaturally wise look.

The older man of the party here interposed with an admonitory warning:

"Now, boys, I advise you to keep out of these oriental scraps. We don't want to get mixed up in any teahouse brawls. These Japanese girls are used——"

"She's not a Japanese girl," furiously denied Jerry. "She's as white as we are. Did you see her hair?"

"Nevertheless——" began Professor Barrowes, but was instantly silenced by his clamouring young charges.

"I," said Jerry, "propose to go on a privately conducted tour of investigation into the infernal regions of that house of alleged joys. If any of you fellows have cold feet, stay right here snug with papa. I'll go it alone."

That was quite enough for the impetuous youngsters. With a whoop of derision at the idea of their having "cold feet," they were soon following Jerry in a rush upon the house that was reminiscent of football days.

In the main hall of the teahouse a bevy of girls were running about agitatedly, some of them with their sleeves before their faces, crying. Two little apprentices crouched up against a screen, loudly moaning. There was every evidence of upset and distress in the House of a Thousand Joys. To Jerry's demand for Hirata, he was met by a frightened silence from the girls, and a stony faced, sinister-eyed woman attempted to block the passage of the young men, thus unconsciously revealing the direction Hirata had gone. Instantly Jerry was upon the screen and with rough hand had shoved it aside. They penetrated to an interior room that opened upon an outbuilding, which was strung out like a pavilion across the garden. At the end of this long, empty structure, lit only by a single lantern, the Americans found what they sought. Kneeling on the floor, in her skin tights, her hands tied behind her with red cords that cut into the delicate flesh, was the girl who had danced on the rope. Through the thin silk of her tights showed a red welt where one stroke of the lash had fallen. Before her, squatting on his heels, Hirata, one hand holding the whip, and the other his suspended pipe, was waiting for his slave to come to terms. She had felt the first stroke of the lash. It should be her first or last, according to her promise.

As the Americans broke into the apartment, Hirata arose partly to his knees and then to his feet, and as he realized their intention, he began to leap up and down shouting lustily:

"Oi!—Oi! Oi-i-i-!"

Jerry's fist found him under the chin, and silenced him. With murmurs of sympathy and anger, the young men cut the bonds of the little girl. She fell limply upon the floor, breathlessly sighing:

"Arigato! Arigato! Arigato!" (Thank you.)

"Hustle. Did you hear that gong! They're summoning the police. Let's beat it."

"And leave her here at his mercy? Nothing doing."

Jerry had lifted the child bodily in his arms, and tossed her across his shoulder. They came out of the house and the gardens through a hue and cry of alarmed attendants and inmates. Hirata had crawled on hands and knees into the main dance hall, and every drum was beating upon the place. Above the beat of the drums came the shrill outcry of Hirata, yelling at the top of his voice:

"Hotogoroshi!" (Murder.)

Through a protecting lane made by his friends, fled Jerry Hammond, the girl upon his shoulder, a chattering, clattering, screeching mob at his heels, out of the gardens and into the dusky streets, under the benignant eye of the Lady Moon, in whose honour a thousand revellers and banquetters were celebrating. Fleet of foot and strong as a young Atlas, Jerry, buoyed up with excitement and rage, fled like the wind before his pursuers, till presently he came to the big brick house, the building of which had been such a source of wonder and amusement to the Japanese, but which had ever afterwards housed white residents sojourning in the city. With one foot Jerry kicked peremptorily upon the door, and a moment later a startled young Japanese butler flung the heavy doors apart, and Jerry rushed in.

CHAPTER II

She awoke on a great soft bed that seemed to her wondering eyes as large as a room. She was sunk in a veritable nest of down, and, sitting up, she put out a little cautious hand and felt and punched the great pillow to reassure herself as to its reality. There was a vague question trembling in the girl's mind as to whether she might not, in fact, have escaped from Hirata through the same medium as her adored mother, and was now being wafted on a snowy cloud along the eternal road to Nirvanna.

Then the small statue like figure at the foot of the great mahogany bed moved. Memory flooded the girl. She thought of her mother, and a sob of anguish escaped her. Crowding upon the mother came the memory of that delirious moment upon the rope, when feeling that her mother's spirit was animating her body, she had faced the revellers. Followed the shivering thought of Hirata—the lash upon her shoulder, its sting paining so that the mere recollection caused her face to blanch with terror, dissipated by the memory of what had followed. Again she felt the exciting thrill of that long flight through the night on the shoulder of the strange young barbarian. He had burst into the room like a veritable god from the heavens, and it was impossible to think of him otherwise than some mighty spirit which the gods had sent to rescue and save the unworthy child of the dancer. In an instant, she was out of bed, her quick glance searching the big room, as if somewhere within it her benefactor was. She was still in her sadly ragged tights, the red welt showing where the silk had been split by the whip of Hirata.

The maid approached and wrapped the girl in one of her own kimonas. She was a silent tongued, still faced woman, who spoke not at all as she swiftly robed her charge. A servant in the household of the Americans, she had been summoned in the night to attend the strange new visitor. Goto, the house boy, had explained to Hatsu that the girl was a dancer from a neighbouring teahouse, whom his young masters had kidnapped. She was a great prize, jealously to be guarded, whispered the awed and gossiping Goto. Hatsu at first had her doubts on this score, for no dancer or teahouse maiden within her knowledge had ever worn hair of such a colour nor had skin which was bleached as that of the dead. Hatsu had discovered her charge in a sleep of complete exhaustion, her soft fair hair tossed about her on the pillow like that of a child.

Now as the maid removed the tawdry tights, and arrayed the strange girl in a respectable kimona, she recognised that those shapely and supple limbs could only be the peculiar heritage of a dancer and performer. A warmth radiated lovingly through her hands as she dressed the young creature confided to her charge. It had never been the lot of Hatsu to serve one as beautiful as this girl, and there was something of maternal pride in her as she fell to her task. There was necessity for haste, for the "Mr. American sirs" were assembled in the main room awaiting her. Hatsu's task completed, she took the girl by the sleeve, and led her into the big living room, where were her friends.

Even in the long loose robes of the elderly maid, she appeared but a child, with her short hair curling about her face, and her frankly questioning eyes turning from one to the other. There was an expression of mingled appeal and childish delight in that expressive look that she turned upon them ere she knelt on the floor. She made her obeisances with art and grace, as a true apprentice of her mother. Indeed, her head ceased not to bob till a laughing young voice broke the spell of silence that her advent had caused with:

"Cut it out, kid! We want to have a look at you. Want to see what sort of prize we pulled in the dark."

Promptly, obediently she rested back upon her heels, her two small hands resting flatly on her knees. She turned her face archly, as if inviting inspection, much to the entertainment of the now charmed circle. The apprentice of the House of a Thousand Joys upheld the prestige of her mother's charm. Even the thin, elderly man, with the bright glasses over which he seemed to peer with an evidently critical and appraising air, softened visibly before that mingled look of naïve appeal and glowing youth. The glasses were blinked from the nose, and dangled by their gold string. He approached nearer to the girl, again put on his glasses, and subjected her through them to a searching scrutiny, his trained eye resting longer upon the shining hair of the girl. The glasses blinked off again at the unabashed wide smile of confidence in those extraordinary eyes; he cleared his throat, prepared to deliver an opinion and diagnosis upon the particular species before his glass. Before he could speak, Jerry broke in belligerently.

"First of all, let's get this thing clear. She's not going to be handed back to that blanketty blank baboon. I'm responsible for her, and I'm going to see that she gets a square deal from this time on."

The girl's eyes widened as she looked steadily at the kindling face of the young man, whom she was more than ever assured was a special instrument of the gods. Professor Barrowes cleared his throat noisily again, and holding his glasses in his hand, punctuated and emphasised his remarks:

"Young gentlemen, I suggest that we put the matter in the hands of Mr. Blumenthal, our consul here at Nagasaki. I do not know—I will not express—my opinion of what our rights are in the matter—er as to whether we have in fact broken some law of Japan in—er—thus forcibly bringing the—ah—young lady to our home. I am inclined to think that we are about to experience trouble—considerable trouble I should say—with this man Hirata. If my memory serves me right, I recall hearing or reading somewhere that a master of such a house has certain property right in these—er—young—ah—ladies."

"That may be true," admitted the especial agent of the gods. "Suppose she is owned by this man. I'll bet that Japan is not so dashed mediæval in its laws, that it permits a chimpanzee like that to beat and ill-use even a slave, and anyway, we'll give him all that's coming to him if he tries to take her from us."

"He'll have his hands danged full trying!"

The girl's champion this time was the youthful one of the bone ribbed glasses. Looking at him very gravely, she perceived his amazing youth, despite the wise spectacles that had at first deceived her. There was that about him that made her feel he was very near to her own age, which numbered less than fifteen years. Across the intervening space between them, hazily the girl thought, what a charming playmate the boy of the bone ribbed glasses would make. She would have liked to run through the temple gardens with him, and hide in the cavities of the fantastic rocks, where Japanese children loved to play, and where the wistful eyes of the solitary little apprentice of the House of a Thousand Joys had often longingly and enviously watched them. Her new friend she was to know as "Monty." He had a fine long name with a junior on the end of it also, but it took many years before she knew her friends by other than the appellations assigned to them by each other.

Now the elderly man—perhaps he was the father, thought the girl on the mat—was again speaking in that emphatic tone of authority.

"Now my young friends, we have come to Japan with a view to studying the country and people, and to avail ourselves of such pleasures as the country affords to its tourists, etc., and, I may point out, that it was no part of our programme or itinerary to take upon ourselves the responsibility and burden, I may say, of———"

"Have—a heart!"

The big slow voice came from the very fat young man, whose melancholy expression belied the popular conception of the comical element associated with those blessed with excessive flesh. "Jinx," as his chums called him, was the scion of a house of vast wealth and fame, and it was no fault of his that his heritage had been rich also in fat, flesh and bone. But now the girl's first friend, with that manner of the natural leader among men, had again taken matters into his own evidently competent hands.

"I say, Jinx, suppose you beat it over to the consul's and get what advice and dope you can from him. Tell him we purpose carrying the case to Washington and so forth. And you, Monty and Bobs, skin over to the teahouse and scare the guts out of that chimpanzee. Hire a bunch of Japs and cops to help along with the noise. Give him the scare of his life. Tell him she—she is—dying—at her last gasp and——"

(Surely the object of their concern understood the English language, for just then several unexpected dimples sprang abroad, and the little row of white teeth showed that smile that was her heritage from her mother.)

"Tell him," went on Jerry, a bit unevenly, deviated from his single track of thought by that most engaging and surprising smile—"that we'll have him boiled in oil or lava or some other Japanese concoction. Toddle along, old dears, or that fellow with the face supporting the Darwinian theory will get ahead of us with the police."

"What's your hurry?" growled Jinx, his sentimental gaze resting fascinatedly upon the girl on the floor.

The young man Jerry had referred to as Bobs now suggested that there was a possibility that the girl was deaf and dumb, in view of the fact that she had not spoken once. This alarming suggestion created ludicrous consternation.

"Where's that dictionary, confound it!" Jerry sought the elusive book in sundry portions of his clothing, and then appealed to the oracle of the party.

"I suggest," said Professor Barrowes didactically, "that you try the—ah—young lady—with the common Japanese greeting. I believe you all have learned it by now."

Promptly there issued from four American mouths the musical morning greeting of the Japanese, reminiscent to them of a well known State productive of presidents.

"O—hi—o!"

The effect on the girl was instantaneous. She arose with grace to her feet, put her two small hands on her two small knees, bobbed up and down half a dozen times, and then with that white row of pearls revealed in an irresistible smile, she returned:

"Goog—a—morning!"

There was a swelling of chests at this. Pride in their protégé aroused them to enthusiastic expressions.

"Can you beat it?"

"Did you hear her?"

"She's a cute kid."

And from Monty:

"I could have told you from the first that a girl with hair and eyes like that wouldn't be chattering any monkey speech."

Thereupon the girl, uttered another jewel in English, which called forth not merely approbation, but loud and continuous applause, laughter, and fists clapped into hands. Said the girl:

"I speag those mos' bes' Angleesh ad Japan!"

"I'll say you do," agreed Monty with enthusiasm.

"Gosh!" said Jinx sadly. "She's the cutest kid *I've* ever seen."

"How old are you?" Jerry put the question gently, touched, despite the merriment her words had occasioned, by something forlorn in the little figure on the mat before them, so evidently anxious to please them.

"How ole?" Her expressive face showed evidence of deep regret at having to admit the humiliating fact that her years numbered but fourteen and ten months. She was careful to add the ten months to the sum of her years.

"And what's your name?"

"I are got two names."

"We all have that—Christian and surname we call 'em. What's yours?"

"I are got Angleesh name—Fleese. You know those name?" she inquired anxiously. "Thas Angleesh name."

"Fleese! Fleese!" Not one of them but wanted to assure her that "Fleese" was a well known name in the English tongue, but even Professor Barrowes, an authority on the roots of all names, found "Fleese" a new one. She was evidently disappointed, and said in a slightly depressed voice:

- 11 -

"I are sawry you do not know thad Angleesh name. My father are give me those name."

"I have it! I have it!" Bobs, who had been scribbling something on paper, and repeating it with several accents, shouted that the name the girl meant was undoubtedly "Phyllis," and at that she nodded her head so vigorously, overjoyed that he threw back his head and burst into laughter, which was loudly and most joyously and ingenuously entered into by "Phyllis" also.

"So that's your name—Phyllis," said Jerry. "You *are* English then?"

She shook her head, sighing with regret.

"No, I sawry for those. I *lig'* be Angleesh. Thas nize be Angleesh; but me, I are not those. Also I are got Japanese name. It are Sunlight. My mother———" Her face became instantly serious as she mentioned her mother, and bowed her head to the floor reverently. "My honourable mother have give me that Japanese name—Sunlight, but my father are change those name. He are call me—Sunny. This whad he call me when he go away———" Her voice trailed off forlornly, hurt by a memory that went back to her fifth year.

They wanted to see her smile again, and Jerry cried enthusiastically:

"Sunny! Sunny! What a corking little name! It sounds just like you look. We'll call you that too—Sunny."

Now Professor Barrowes, too long in the background, came to the fore with precision. He had been scratching upon a pad of paper a number of questions he purposed to put to Sunny, as she was henceforth to be known to her friends.

"I have a few questions I desire to ask the young—ah—lady, if you have no objection. I consider it advisable for us to ascertain what we properly can about the history of Miss—er—Sunny—and so, if you will allow me."

He cleared his throat, referred to the paper in his hand and propounded the first question as follows:

"Question number one: Are you a white or a Japanese girl?"

Answer from Sunny:

"I are white on my face and my honourable body, but I are Japanese on my honourable insides."

Muffled mirth followed this reply, and Professor Barrowes having both blown his nose and cleared his throat applied his glasses to his nose but was obliged to wait a while before resuming, and then:

"Question number two: Who were or are your parents? Japanese or white people?"

Sunny, her cheeks very red and her eyes very bright:

"Aexcuse me. I are god no parents or ancestors on those worl'. I sawry. I miserable girl wizout no ancestor."

"Question number three: You had parents. You remember them. What nationality was your mother? I believe Madame Many Smiles was merely her professional pseudonym. I have heard her variously described as white, partly white, half caste. What was she—a white woman or a Japanese?"

Sunny was thinking of that radiant little mother as last she had seen her in the brilliant dancing robes of the dead geisha. The questions were touching the throbbing cords of a memory that pierced. Over the sweet young face a shadow crept.

"My m-mother," said Sunny softly, "are god two bloods ad her insides. Her father are Lussian gentleman and her mother are Japanese."

"And your father?"

A far-away look came into the girl's eyes as she searched painfully back into that past that held such sharply bright and poignantly sad memories of the father she had known such a little time. She no longer saw the eager young faces about her, or the kindly one of the man who questioned her. Sunny was looking out before her across the years into that beautiful past, wherein among the cherry blossoms she had wandered with her father. It was he who had changed her Japanese name of Sunlight to "Sunny." A psychologist might have found in this somewhat to redeem him from his sins against his child and her mother, for surely the name revealed a softness of the heart which his subsequent conduct might have led a sceptical world to doubt. Moreover, the first language of her baby lips was that of her father, and for five years she knew no other tongue. She thought of him always as of some gay figure in a bright dream that fled away suddenly into the cruel years that followed. There had been days of real terror and fear, when Sunny and her mother had taken the long trail of the mendicant, and knew what it was to feel hunger and cold and the chilly hand of charity. The mere memory of those days set the girl shivering, for it seemed such a short time since when she and that dearest mother crouched outside houses that, lighted within, shone warmly, like gaudy paper lanterns in the night; of still darker days of discomfort and misery, when they had hidden in bush, bramble and in dark woods beyond the paths of men. There had been a period of sweet rest and refuge in a mountain temple. There everything had appealed to the imaginative child. Tinkling bells and whirring wings of a thousand doves, whose home was in gilded loft and spire; bald heads of murmuring bonzes; waving sleeves of the visiting priestesses, dancing before the shrine to please the gods; the weary pilgrims who climbed to the mountain's heart to throw their prayers in the lap of the peaceful Buddha. A hermitage in a still wood, where an old, old nun, with gentle feeble voice, crooned over her rosary. All this was as a song that lingers in one's ears long after the melody has passed—a memory that stung with its very sweetness. Even here the fugitives were not permitted to linger for long.

Pursuing shadows haunted her mother's footsteps and sent her speeding ever on. She told her child that the shadows menaced their safety. They had come from across the west ocean, said the mother. They were barbarian thieves of the night, whose mission was to separate mother from child, and because separation from her mother spelled for little Sunny a doom more awful than death itself, she was wont to smother back her child's cries in her sleeve, and bravely and silently push onward. So for a period of time of which neither mother nor child took reckoning the days of their vagabondage passed.

Then came a night when they skirted the edges of a city of many lights; lights that hung like stars in the sky; lights that swung over the intricate canals that ran into streets in and out of the city; harbour lights from great ships that steamed into the port; the countless little lights of junks and fisher boats, and the merry lights that shone warmly inside the pretty paper houses that bespoke home and rest to the outcasts. And they came to a brilliantly lighted garden, where on long poles and lines the lanterns were strung, and within the gates they heard the chattering of the drum, and the sweet tinkle of the samisen. Here at the gates of the House of a Thousand Joys the mother touched the gongs. A man with a lantern in his hand came down to the gates, and as the woman spoke, he raised the light till it revealed that delicate face, whose loveliness neither pain nor privation nor time nor even death had ravaged.

After that, the story of the geisha was well known. Her career had been an exceptional one in that port of many teahouses. From the night of her début to the night of her death the renown of Madame Many Smiles had been undimmed.

Sunny, looking out before her, in a sad study, that caught her up into the web of the vanished years, could only shake her head dumbly at her questioner, as he pressed her:

"Your father—you have not answered me?"

"I kinnod speag about my—father. I sawry, honourable sir," and suddenly the child's face drooped forward as if she humbly bowed, but the young men watching her saw the tears that dropped on her clasped hands.

Exclamations of pity and wrath burst from them impetuously.

"We've no right to question her like this," declared Jerry Hammond hotly. "It's not of any consequence who her people are. She's got us now. We'll take care of her from this time forth." At that Sunny again raised her head, and right through her tears she smiled up at Jerry. It made him think of an April shower, the soft rain falling through the sunlight.

CHAPTER III

Only one who has been in bondage all of his days can appreciate that thrill that comes with sudden freedom. The Americans had set Sunny free. She had been bound by law to the man Hirata through an iniquitous bond that covered all the days of her young life—a bond into which the average geisha is sold in her youth. Sunny's mother had signed the contract when starvation faced them, and reassured by the promises of Hirata.

What price and terms the avaricious Hirata extracted from the Americans is immaterial, but they took precautions that the proceeding should be in strict accord with the legal requirements of Japan. The American consul and Japanese lawyers governed the transaction. Hirata, gloated with the unexpected fortune that had come to him through the sale of the apprentice-geisha, overwhelmed the disgusted young men, whom he termed now his benefactors, with servile compliments, and hastened to comply with all their demands, which included the delivery to Sunny of the effects of her mother. Goto bore the box containing her mother's precious robes and personal belongings into the great living room.

Life had danced by so swiftly and strangely for Sunny in these latter days, that she had been diverted from her sorrow. Now, as she slowly opened the bamboo chest, with its intangible odour of dear things, she experienced a strangling sense of utter loss and pain. Never again would she hear that gentle voice, admonishing and teaching her; never again would she rest her tired head on her mother's knee and find rest and comfort from the sore trials of the day; for the training of the apprentice-geisha is harsh and spartan like. As Sunny lifted out her mother's sparkling robe, almost she seemed to see the delicate head above it. A sob broke from the heart of the girl, and throwing herself on the floor by the chest, she wept with her face in the silken folds. A moth fluttered out of one of the sleeves, and hung tremulously above the girl's head. Sunny, looking up, addressed it reverently:

"I will not hurt you, little moth. It may be you are the spirit of my honourable mother. Pray you go upon your way," and she softly blew up at the moth.

It was that element of helplessness, a feminine quality of appeal about Sunny, that touched something in the hearts of her American friends that was chivalrous and quixotic. Always, when Sunny was in trouble, they took the jocular way of expressing their feelings for their charge. To tease, joke, chaff and play with Sunny, that was their way. So, on this day, when they returned to the house, to find the girl with her tear-wet face pressed against her mother's things, they sought an instant means, and as Jerry insisted, a practical one, of banishing her sadness. After the box had been taken from the room, Goto and Jinx told some funny stories, which brought a faint smile to Sunny's face. Monty proffered a handful of sweets picked up in some adjacent shop, while Bobs sought scientifically to arouse her to a semblance of her buoyant spirits by discussing all the small live things that were an unfailing source of interest always to the girl, and pretended an enthusiasm over white rabbits which he declared were in the garden. Jerry broached his marvellous plan, pronounced by Professor Barrowes to be preposterous, unheard of and impossible. In Jerry's own words, the scheme was as follows:

"I propose that we organise and found a company or Syndicate, all present to have the privilege of owning stock in said company; its purpose being to take care of Sunny for the rest of her days. Sooner or later we fellows must return to the U. S. We are going to provide for Sunny's future after we are gone."

Thus the Sunny Syndicate Limited came into being. It was capitalised at $10,000, paid in capital, a considerable sum in Japan, and quite sufficient to keep the girl in comfort for the rest of her days. Professor Timothy Barrowes was unanimously elected President, J. Lyon Crawford (Jinx) treasurer; Robert M. Mapson (Bobs), secretary of the concern, and Joseph Lamont Potter, Jr. (Monty), though under age, after an indignant argument was permitted to hold a minimum measure of stock and also voted a director. J. Addison Hammond, Jr. (Jerry), held down the positions of first vice-president, managing director and general manager and was grudgingly admitted to be the founder and promoter of the great idea, and the discoverer of Sunny, assets of aforesaid Syndicate.

At the initial Board meeting of the Syndicate, which was riotously attended, the purpose of the Syndicate was duly set forth in the minutes read, approved and signed by all, which was, to wit, to feed, clothe, educate and furnish with sundry necessities and luxuries the aforesaid Sunny for the rest of her natural days.

The education of Sunny strongly appealed to the governing president, who, despite his original protest, was the most active member of the Syndicate. He promptly outlined a course which would tend to cultivate those hitherto unexplored portions of Sunny's pliable young mind. A girl of almost fifteen, unable to read or write, was in the opinion of Professor Barrowes a truly benighted heathen. What matter that she knew the Greater Learning for Women by heart, knew the names of all the gods and goddesses cherished by the Island Empire; had an intimate acquaintance with the Japanese language, and was able to translate and indite epistles in the peculiar figures intelligible only to the Japanese. The fact remained that she was in a state of abysmal ignorance so far as American education was concerned. Her friends assured her of the difficulty of their task, and impressed upon her the necessity of hard study and co-operation on her part. She was not merely to learn the American language, she was, with mock seriousness, informed, but she was to acquire the American point of view, and in fact unlearn much of the useless knowledge she had acquired of things Japanese.

To each member of the Syndicate Professor Barrowes assigned a subject in which he was to instruct Sunny. Himself he appointed principal of the "seminary" as the young men merrily named it; Jerry was instructor in reading and writing, Bobs in spelling, Jinx in arithmetic, and to young Monty, aged seventeen, was intrusted the task of instructing Sunny in geography, a subject Professor Barrowes well knew the boy was himself deficient in. He considered this an ideal opportunity, in a sort of inverted way, to instruct Monty himself. To the aid and help of the Americans came the Reverend Simon Sutherland, a missionary, whose many years of service among the heathen had given to his face that sadly solemn expression of martyr zealot. His the task to transform Sunny into a respectable Christian girl.

Sunny's progress in her studies was eccentric. There were times when she was able to read so glibly and well that the pride of her teacher was only dashed when he discovered that she had somehow learned the words by heart, and in picking them out had an exasperating habit of pointing to the wrong words. She could count to ten in English. Her progress in Geography was attested to by her admiring and enthusiastic teacher, and she herself, dimpling, referred to the U. S. A. as being "over cross those west water, wiz grade flag of striped stars."

However, her advance in religion exceeded all her other attainments, and filled the breast of the good missionary with inordinate pride. An expert and professional in the art of converting the heathen, he considered Sunny's conversion at the end of the second week as little short of miraculous, and, as he explained to the generous young Americans, who had done so much for the mission school in which the Reverend Simon Sutherland was interested, he was of the opinion that the girl's quick comprehension of the religion was due to a sort of reversion to type, she being mainly of white blood. So infatuated indeed was the good man by his pupil's progress that he could not forbear to bring her before her friends, and show them what prayer and sincere labour among the heathen were capable of doing.

Accordingly, the willing and joyous convert was haled before an admiring if somewhat sceptical circle in the cheerful living room of the Americans. Here, her hands clasped piously together, she chanted the prepared formula:

"Gentlemens"—Familiar daily intercourse with her friends brought easily to the girl's tongue their various nicknames, but "Gentlemens" she now addressed them.

"I stan here to make statements to you that I am turn Kirishitan."

"English, my dear child. Use the English language, please."

"—that I am turn those Christian girl. I can sing those—a-gospel song; and I are speak those—ah—gospel prayer, and I know those cat—cattykussem like—like——"

Sunny wavered as she caught the uplifted eyebrow of the missionary signalling to her behind the back of Professor Barrowes. Now the words began to fade away from Sunny. Alone with the missionary it was remarkable how quickly she was able to commit things to memory. Before an audience like this, she was as a child who stands upon a platform with his first recitation, and finds his tongue tied and memory failing. What was it now the Reverend Simon Sutherland desired her to say? Confused, but by no means daunted, Sunny cast about in her mind for some method of propitiating the minister. At least, she could pray. Folding her hands before her, and dropping her Buddhist rosary through her fingers, she murmured the words of that quaint old hymn:

"What though those icy breeze,He blow sof' on ze isleThough evrything he pleasesAnd jos those man he's wild,In vain with large kindThe gift of those gods are sown,Those heathen in blindnessBow down to wood and stone."

They let her finish the chant, the words of which were almost unintelligible to her convulsed audience, who vainly sought to strangle their mirth before the crestfallen and sadly hurt Mr. Sutherland. He took the rosary from Sunny's fingers, saying reprovingly:

"My dear child, that is not a prayer, and how many times must I tell you that we do not use a rosary in our church. All we desire from you at this time is a humble profession as to your conversion to Christianity. Therefore, my child, your friends and I wish to be reassured on that score."

"I'd like to hear her do the catechism. She says she knows it," came in a muffled voice from Bobs.

"Certainly, certainly," responded the missionary. "Attention, my dear. First, I will ask you: What is your name?"

Sunny, watching him with the most painful earnestness indicative of her earnest desire to please, was able to answer at once joyously.

"My name are Sunny—Syndicutt."

The mirth was barely suppressed by the now indignant minister, who glared in displeasure upon the small person so painfully trying to realise his ambitions for her. To conciliate the evidently angry Mr. Sutherland, she rattled along hurriedly:

"I am true convert. I swear him. By those eight million gods of the heavens and the sea, and by God-dam I swear it that I am nixe Kirishitan girl."

A few minutes later Sunny was alone, even Professor Barrowes having hastily followed his charges from the room to avoid giving offence to the missionary, whose angry tongue was now loosened, and flayed the unhappy girl ere he too departed in dudgeon via the front door.

That evening, after the dinner, Sunny, who had been very quiet during the meal, went directly from the table to her room upstairs, and to the calls after her of her friends, she replied that she had "five thousan words to learn him to spell."

Professor Barrowes, furtively wiping his eyes and then his glasses, shook them at his protesting young charges and asserted that the missionary was quite within his rights in punishing Sunny by giving her 500 lines to write.

"She's been at it all day," was the disgusted comment of Monty. "It's a rotten shame, to put that poor kid to copying that little hell of a line."

"Sir," said the Professor, stiffening and glaring through his glasses at Monty, "I wish you to know that line happens to be taken from a—er—book esteemed sacred, and I have yet to learn that it had its origin in the infernal regions as suggested by you. What is more, I may say that Miss Sunny's progress in reading and spelling, arithmetic, and geography has not been what I had hoped. Accordingly I have instructed her that she must study for an hour in the evening after dinner, and I have further advised the young lady that I do not wish her to leave the house on any pleasure expedition this evening."

A howl of indignant protest greeted this pronouncement and the air was electric with bristling young heads.

"Say, Proff. Sunny promised to go out with me this evening. She knows a shop where they sell that sticky gum drop stuff that I like, and we're going down Snowdrop Ave. to Canal Lane. Let her off, just this time, will you?"

"I will not. She must learn to spell Cat, Cow, Horse and Dog and such words as a baby of five knows properly before she can go out on pleasure trips."

Jinx ponderously sat up on his favourite sofa, the same creaking under him as the big fellow moved. In an injured tone he set forth his rights for the evening to Sunny.

"Sunny has a date with me to play me a nice little sing-song on that Jap guitar of hers. I'm not letting her off this or any other night."

"She made a date with me too," laughed Bobs. "We were to star gaze, if you please. She says she knows the history of all the most famous stars in the heavens, and she agreed to show me the exact geographical spot in the firmament where that Amaterumtumtum, or whatever she calls it, goddess, lost her robes in the Milky Way just while she was descending to earth to be an ancestor to the Emperor of Japan." Mockingly Bobs bowed his head in solemn and comical imitation of Sunny at the mention of the Emperor.

Jerry was thinking irritably that Sunny and he were to have stolen away after supper for a little trip in a private junk, owned by a friend of Sunny's, and she said that the rowers would play the guitar and sing as the gondoliers of Italy do. Jerry had a fancy for that trip in the moonlight, with Sunny's little hand cuddled up in his, and the child chattering some of her pretty nonsense. Confound it, the little baggage had promised her time to every last one of her friends, and so it was nearly every night in the week. Sunny had much ado making and breaking engagements with her friends.

"It strikes me," said Professor Barrowes, stroking his chin humorously, "that Miss Sunny has in her all the elements that go to the making of a most complete and finished coquette. For your possible edification, gentlemen, I will mention that the young lady also offered to accompany me to a certain small temple where she informs me a bonze of the Buddhist religion has a library of er—one million years, so claims Miss Sunny, and this same bonze she assured me has a unique collection of ancient butterflies which have come down from prehistoric days. Ahem!—er—I shall play fair with you young gentlemen. I desire very much to see the articles I have mentioned. I doubt very much the authenticity of the same, but have an open mind. I shall, however, reserve the pleasure of seeing these collections till a more convenient period. In the meanwhile I advise you all to go about your respective concerns, and I bid you good-night, gentlemen, I bid you good-night."

The house was silent. The living room, with its single reading lamp, seemed empty and cold, and Professor Barrowes with a book whose contents would have aforetime utterly absorbed him, as it dealt with the fascinating subject of the Dinornis, of post-Pliocene days, found himself unable to concentrate. His well-governed mind had in some inexplicable way become intractable. It persisted in wandering up to the floor above, where Professor Barrowes knew was a poor young girl, who was studying hard into the night. Twice he went outdoors to assure himself that Sunny was still studying, and each time the glowing light, and the chanting voice aroused his further compunction and remorse. Unable longer to endure the distracting influence that took his mind from his favourite study, the Professor stole on tiptoe up the stairs to Sunny's door. The voice inside went raucously on.

"C-a-t—dog. C-a-t—dog. C-a-t—dog!"

Something about that voice, devoid of all the charm peculiar to Sunny, grated against the sensitive ear at the keyhole, and accordingly he withdrew the ear and applied the eye. What he saw inside caused him to sit back solidly on the floor, speechless with mirthful indignation.

Hatsu, the maid, sat stonily before the little desk of her mistress, and true to the instructions of Sunny, she was loudly chanting that C-a-t spelled Dog.

Outside the window—well, there was a lattice work that ascended conveniently to Sunny's room. Her mode of exit was visible to the simplest minded, but the question that agitated the mind of Professor Barrowes, and sent him off into a spree of mirthful speculation was which one of the members of the Sunny Syndicate Limited had Miss Sunny Sindicutt eloped with?

CHAPTER IV

To be adopted by four young men and one older one; to be surrounded by every care and luxury; to be alternately scolded, pampered, admonished and petted, this was the joyous fate of Sunny. Life ran along for the happy child like a song, a poem which even Takumushi could not have composed.

Sunny greeted the rising sun with the kisses that she had been taught to throw to garden audiences, and hailed the blazing orb each morning, having bowed three times, hands on knees, with words like these:

"Ohayo! honourable Sun. I glad you come again. Thas a beautiful day you are bring, an I thang you thad I are permit to live on those day. Hoh! Amaterasuoho-mikami, shining lady of the Sun, I are mos' happiest girl ad those Japan!"

The professional geisha is taught from childhood—for her apprenticeship begins from earliest youth—that her mission in life is to bring joy and happiness into the world, to divert, to banish all care by her own infectious buoyancy, to heal, to dissipate the cares of mere mortals; to cultivate herself so that she shall become the very essence of joy. If trouble comes to her own life, to so exercise self-control that no trace of her inner distress must be reflected in her looks or conduct. She must, in fact, make a science of her profession. To laugh with those who laugh and weep with those who find a balm in tears—that is the work of the geisha.

Sunny, a product of the geisha house, and herself apprentice to the joy women of Japan, was of another race by blood, yet always there was to cling to her that intangible charm, that like a strange perfume bespeaks the geisha of Japan. In her odd way Sunny laid out her campaign to charm and please the ones who had befriended her, and toward whom she felt a gratitude that both touched and embarrassed them.

Her new plan of life, however, violated all the old rules which had governed in the teahouse. Sunny was sore put to it to adjust herself to the novelty of a life that knew not the sharp and imperative voice, which cut like a whip in staccato order, from the master of the geishas; nor the perilous trapeze, the swinging rope, to fall from which was to bring down upon her head harsh rebuke, and sometimes the threatening flash of the whip, whirling in the air, and barely scraping the girl on the rope. She had been whipped but upon that one occasion, for her mother was too valuable an asset in the House of a Thousand Joys for Hirata to risk offending; but always he loved to swing the lash above the girl's head, or hurl it near to the feet that had faltered from the rope, so that she might know that it hung suspended above her to fall at a time when she failed. There were pleasant things too in the House of a Thousand Smiles that Sunny missed—the tap tap of the drum, the pat pat of the stockinged feet on the polished dance matting; the rising and falling of the music of the samisen as it tinkled in time to the swaying fans and posturing bodies of the geishas. All this was the joyous part of that gaudy past, which her honourable new owners had bidden her forget.

Sunny desired most earnestly to repay her benefactors, but her offers to dance for them were laughingly joshed aside, and she was told that they did not wish to be repaid in dancing coin. All they desired in return was that she should be happy, forget the bitter past, and they always added "grow up to be the most beautiful girl in Japan." This was a joking formula among them. To order Sunny to be merely happy and beautiful. Happy she was, but beauty! Ah! that was more difficult.

Beauty, thought Sunny, must surely be the aim and goal of all Americans. Many were the moments when she studied her small face in the mirror, and regretted that it would be impossible for her to realise the ambition of her friends. Her face, she was assured, violated all the traditions and canons of the Japanese ideal of beauty. That required jet black hair, lustrous as lacquer, a long oval face, with tiny, carmine touched lips, narrow, inscrutable eyes, a straight, sensitive nose, a calmness of expression and poise that should serve as a mask to all internal emotions; above all an elegance and distinction in manners and dress that would mark one as being of an elevated station in life. Now Sunny's hair was fair, and despite brush and oil generously applied, till forbidden by her friends, it curled in disobedient ringlets about her young face. The hair alone marked her in the estimation of the Japanese as akin to the lower races, since curly hair was one of the marks peculiar to the savages. Neither were her eyes according to the Japanese ideal of beauty. They were, it is true, long and shadowed by the blackest of lashes, and in fact were her one feature showing the trace of her oriental taint or alloy, for they tipped up somewhat at the corners, and she had a trick of glancing sideways through the dark lashes that her friends found eerily fascinating; unfortunately those eyes were large, and instead of being the prescribed black, were pure amber in colour, with golden lights of the colour of her hair. Her skin, finally, was, as the mentor of the geisha house had primly told her, bleached like the skin of the dead. Save where the colour flooded her cheeks like peach bloom, Sunny's skin was as white as snow, and all the temporary stains and dark powder applied could not change the colour of her skin. To one accustomed to the Japanese point of view, Sunny therefore could see nothing in her own lovely face that would realise the desire of her friends that she should be beautiful; but respectfully and humbly she promised them that she would try to obey them, and she carried many gifts and offerings to the feet of Amaterasu-ohomikami, whose beauty had made her the supreme goddess of the heavens.

"Beauty," said Jerry Hammond, walking up and down the big living room, his hair rumpled, and his hands loosely in his pockets, "is the aim and end of all that is worth while in life, Sunny. If we have it, we have everything. Beauty is something we are unable to define. It is elusive as a feather that floats above our heads. A breath will blow it beyond our reach, and a miracle will bring it to our hand. Now, the gods willing, I am going to spend all of the days of my life pursuing and reaching after Beauty. Despite my parents' fond expectations of a commercial career for their wayward son, I propose to be an artist."

From which it will be observed that Jerry's idea of beauty was hardly that comprehended by Sunny, though in a vague way she sensed also his ideal.

"An artist!" exclaimed she, clasping her hands with enthusiasm. "Ho! *how* thad will be grade. I thing you be more grade artist than Hokusai!"

"Oh, Sunny, impossible! Hokusai was one of the greatest artists that ever lived. I'm not built of the same timber, Sunny." There was a touch of sadness to Jerry's voice. "My scheme is not to paint pictures. I propose to beautify cities. To the world I shall be known merely as an architect, but you and I, Sunny, we will know, won't we, that I am an artist; because, you see, even if one fails to create the beautiful, the hunger and the desire for it is just as important. It's like being a poet at heart, without being able to write poetry. Now some fellows *write* poetry of a sort—but they are not poets—not in their thought and lives, Sunny. I'd rather be a poet than write poetry. Do you understand that?"

"Yes—I understand," said Sunny softly. "The liddle butterfly when he float on the flower, he cannot write those poetry—but he are a poem; and the honourable cloud in those sky, so sof', so white, so loavely he make one's heart leap up high at chest—thas poem too!"

"Oh, Sunny, what a perfect treasure you are! I'm blessed if you don't understand a fellow better than one of his own countrywomen would."

To cover a feeling of emotion and sentiment that invariably swept over Jerry when he talked with Sunny on the subject of beauty, and because moreover there was that about her own upturned face that disturbed him strangely, he always assumed a mock serious air, and affected to tease her.

"But to get back to you, Sunny. Now, all you've got to do to please the Syndicate is to be a good girl *and* beautiful. It ought not to be hard, because you see you've got such a bully start. Keep on, and who knows you'll end not only by being the most beautiful girl in Japan, but the Emperor himself—the Emperor of Japan, mark you, will step down from his golden throne, wave his wand toward you and marry you! So there you'll be—the royal Empress of Japan."

"The Emperor!" Sunny's head went reverently to the mats. Her eyes, very wide, met Jerry's in shocked question. "You want me marry wiz—the Son of Heaven? *How* I can do those?"

Again her head touched the floor, her curls bobbing against flushed cheeks.

"Easy as fishing," solemnly Jerry assured her. "They say the old dub is quite approachable, and you've only to let him see you once, and that will be enough for him. Just think, Sunny, what that will mean to you, and to us all—to be Empress of Japan. Why, you will only need to wave your hand or sleeve, and all sorts of favours will descend upon our heads. You will be able to repay us threefold for any insignificant service we may have done for you. Once Empress of Japan, you can summon us back to these fair isles and turn over to us all the political plums of the Empire. As soon as you give us the high sign, old scout, we'll be right on the job."

"Jerry, you like very much those plum?"

"You better believe I do."

Sunny, chin in hand, was off in a mood of abstraction. She was thinking very earnestly of the red plum tree that grew above the tomb of the great Lord of Kakodate. He, that sleeping lord, would not miss a single plum, and she would go to the cemetery in the early morning, and when she had accomplished the theft, she would pray at the temple for absolution for her sin, which would not be so bad because Sunny would have sinned for love.

"A penny for your thoughts, Sunny!"

"I are think, Jerry, that some things you ask me I can do; others, no—thas not possible. Wiz this liddle hand I cannod dip up the ocean. Thas proverb of our Japan. I cannod marry those Emperor, and me? I cannod also make beauty on my face."

"Give it a try, Sunny," jeered Jerry, laughing at her serious face. "You have no idea what time and art will do for one."

"Time—and—art," repeated Sunny, like a child learning a lesson. She comprehended time, but she had inherited none of the Japanese traits of patience. She would have wished to leap over that first obstacle to beauty.

Art, she comprehended, as a physical aid to a face and form unendowed with the desired beauty. She carried her problem to her maid.

"Hatsu, have you ever seen the Emperor?"

Both of their heads bobbed quickly to the mat.

Hatsu had not. She had, it is true, walked miles through country roads, on a hot, dry day, to reach the nearest town through which the Son of Heaven's cortege had once passed. But, of course, as the royal party approached, Hatsu, like all the peasants who had come to the town on this gala day, had fallen face downward on the earth. It was impossible for her therefore to see the face of the Son of Heaven. However, Hatsu had seen the back of his horse—the modern Emperor rode thus abroad, clear to the view of subjects less humble than Hatsu, who dared to raise their eyes to his supreme magnificence. Sunny sighed. She felt sure that had she been in Hatsu's place, she would at least have peeped through her fingers at the mikado. Rummaging among her treasures in the bamboo chest, Sunny finally discovered what she sought—a picture of the Emperor. This she laid before her on the floor, and for a long, long time she studied the features thoughtfully and anxiously. After a while, she said with a sigh, unconscious of the blasphemy, which caused her maid to turn pale with horror,

"I do not like his eye, and I do not like his nose, and I do not like his mouth. Yet, Hatsusan, it is the wish of Jerry-sama that I should marry this Emperor, and now I must make myself so beautiful that it will not hurt his eye if he deigns to look at me."

Hatsu, at this moment was too overcome with the utter audacity of the scheme to move, and when she did find her voice, she said in a breathless whisper:

"Mistress, the Son of Heaven already has a wife."

"Ah, yes," returned Sunny, with somewhat of the careless manner toward sacred things acquired from her friends, "but perhaps he may desire another one. Come, Hatsusan. Work very hard on my face. Make me look like ancient picture of an Empress of Japan. See, here is a model!" She offered one of her mother's old prints, that revealed a court lady in trailing gown and loosened hair, an uplifted fan half revealing, half disclosing a weirdly lovely face, as she turned to look at a tiny dog frolicking on her train.

It was a long, a painful and arduous process, this work of beautifying Sunny. There was fractious hair to be darkened and smoothed, and false hair to help out the illusion. There was a small face that had to be almost completely made over, silken robes from the mother's chest to slip over the girlish shoulders, shining nails to be polished and hidden behind gold nail protectors, paint and paste to be thickly applied, and a cape of a thousand colours to be thrown over the voluminous many coloured robes beneath.

The sky was a dazzling blaze of red and gold. Even the deepening shadows were touched with gilt, and the glory of that Japanese sunset cast its reflection upon the book-lined walls of the big living room, where the Americans, lingering over pipe and hook, dreamily and appreciatively watched the marvellous spectacle through the widely opened windows. But their siesta was strangely interrupted, for, like a peacock, a strange vision trailed suddenly into the room and stood with suspended breath, fan half raised, in the manner of a court lady of ancient days, awaiting judgment. They did not know her at first. This strange figure seemed to have stepped out of some old Japanese print, and was as far from being the little Sunny who had come into their lives and added the last touch of magic to their trip in Japan.

After the first shock, they recognised Sunny. Her face was heavily plastered with a white paste. A vivid splotch of red paint adorned and accentuated either slightly high cheek bone. Her eyebrows had disappeared under a thick layer of paste, and in their place appeared a brand new pair of intensely black ones, incongruously laid about an inch above the normal line and midway of her forehead. Her lips were painted to a vivid point, star shaped, so that the paint omitted the corners of Sunny's mouth, where were the dimples that were part of the charm of the Sunny they knew. Upon the girl's head rested an amazing ebony wig, one long lock of which trailed fantastically down from her neck to the hem of her robe. Shining daggers and pins, and artificial flowers completed a head dress. She was arrayed in an antique kimona, an article of stiff and unlimited dimensions, under which were seven other robes of the finest silk, each signifying some special virtue. A train trailed behind Sunny that covered half the length of the room. Her heavily embroidered outer robe was a gift to her mother from a prince, and its magnificence proclaimed its antiquity.

It may be truly said for Sunny that she indeed achieved her own peculiar idea of what constituted beauty, and as she swept the fan from before her face with real art and grace there was pardonable pride in her voice as she said:

"Honourable Mr. sirs, mebbe *now* you goin' say I are beautifullest enough girl to make those Emperor marry wiz me."

A moment of tense silence, and then the room resounded and echoed to the startled mirth of the young barbarians. But no mirth came from Sunny, and no mirth came from Jerry. The girl stood in the middle of the room, and through all her pride and dazzling attire she showed how deeply they had wounded her. A moment only she stayed, and then tripping over her long train and dropping her fan in her hurry, Sunny fled from the room.

Jerry said with an ominous glare at the convulsed Bobs, Monty and even the aforesaid melancholy Jinx:

"It was my fault. I told her art and time would make her beautiful."

"The devil they would," snorted Bobs. "I'd like to know how you figured that art and time could contribute to Sunny's natural beauty. By George, she got herself up with the aid of your damned art, to look like a valentine, if you ask me."

"I don't agree with you," declared Jerry hotly. "It's all how one looks at such things. It's a symptom of provincialism to narrow our admiration to one type only. Such masters as Whistler of our own land, and many of the most famous artists of Europe have not hesitated to take Japanese art as their model. What Sunny accomplished was the reproduction of a living work of art of the past, and it is the crassest kind of ignorance to reward her efforts with laughter."

Jerry was almost savage in his denunciation of his friends.

"I agree with you," said Professor Barrowes snapping his glasses back on his nose, "absolutely, absolutely. You are entirely right, Mr. Hammond," and in turn he glared upon his "class" as if daring anyone of them to question his own opinion. Jinx indeed did feebly say:

"Well, for my part, give me Sunny as we know her. Gosh! I don't see anything pretty in all that dolled-up stuff and paint on her."

"Now, young gentleman," continued Professor Barrowes, seizing the moment to deliver a gratuitous lecture, "there are certain cardinal laws governing art and beauty. It is not a matter of eyes, ears and noses, or even the colour of the skin. It is how we are accustomed to look at a thing. As an example, we might take a picture. Seen from one angle, it reveals a mass of chaotic colour that has no excuse for being. Seen from another point, the purpose of the artist is clearly delineated, and we are trapped in the charm of his creation. Every clime has its own peculiar estimate, but it comes down each time to ourselves. Poetically it has been beautifully expressed as follows: 'Unless we carry the beautiful with us, we will find it not.' Ahem!" Professor Barrowes cleared his throat angrily, and scowled, with Jerry, at their unappreciative friends.

Goto, salaaming deeply in the doorway, was sonorously announcing honourable dinner for the honourable sirs, and coming softly across the hall, in her simple plum coloured kimona with its golden obi, the paint washed from her face, and showing it fresh and clean as a baby's, Sunny's April smile was warming and cheering them all again.

Jinx voiced the sentiment of them all, including the angry professor and beauty loving Jerry:

"Gosh! give me Sunny just as she is, without one plea."

CHAPTER V

There comes a time in the lives of all young men sojourning in foreign lands when the powers that be across the water summon them to return to the land of their birth.

Years before, letters and cablegrams not unsimilar to those that now poured in upon her friends came persistently across the water to the father of Sunny. Then there was no Professor Barrowes to govern and lay down the law to the infatuated man. He was able to put off the departure for several years, but with the passage of time the letters that admonished and threatened not only ceased to come, but the necessary remittances stopped also. Sunny's father found himself in the novel position of being what he termed "broke" in a strange land.

As in the case of Jerry Hammond, whose people were all in trade, there was a strange vein of sentiment in the father of Sunny. To his people indeed, he appeared to be one of those freaks of nature that sometimes appear in the best regulated families, and deviate from the proper paths followed by his forbears. He had acquired a sentiment not merely for the land, but for the woman he had taken as his wife; above all, he was devoted to his little girl. It is hard to judge of the man from his subsequent conduct upon his return to America. His marriage to the mother of Sunny had been more or less of a mercenary transaction. She had been sold to the American by a stepfather anxious to rid himself of a child who showed the clear evidence of her white father, and greedy to avail himself of the terms offered by the American. It was, in fact, a gay union into which the rich, fast young man thoughtlessly entered, with a cynical disregard of anything but his own desires. The result was to breed in him at the outset a feeling that he would not have analysed as contempt, but was at all events scepticism for the seeming love of his wife for him.

It was different with his child. His affection for her was a beautiful thing. No shadow of doubt or criticism came to mar the love that existed between father and child. True, Sunny was the product of a temporary union, a ceremony of the teacup, which nevertheless is a legal marriage in Japan, and so regarded by the Japanese. Lightly as the American may have regarded his union with her mother, he looked upon the child as legally and fully his own, and was prepared to defend her rights.

In America, making a clean breast to parents and family lawyers, he assented to the terms made by them, on condition that his child at least should be obtained for him. The determination to obtain possession of his child became almost a monomania with the man, and he took measures that were undeniably ruthless to gratify his will. It may be also that he was at this time the victim of agents and interested parties. However, he had lived in Japan long enough to know of the proverbial frailty of the sex. The mercenary motives he believed animated the woman in marrying him, her inability to reveal her emotions in the manner of the women of his own race; her seeming indifference and coldness at parting, which indeed was part of her spartan heritage to face dire trouble unblenching—the sort of thing which causes Japanese women to send their warrior husbands into battle with smiles upon their lips—all these things contributed to beat the man into a mood of acquiescence to the demands of his parents. He deluded himself into believing that his Japanese wife, like her dolls, was incapable of any intense feeling.

In due time, the machinery of law, which works for those who pay, with miraculous swiftness in Japan, was set into motion, and the frail bonds that so lightly bound the American to his Japanese wife, were severed. At this time the mother of Sunny had been plastic and apparently complacent, though rejecting the compensation proffered her by her husband's agents. The woman, who was later to be known as Madame Many Smiles, turned cold as death, however, when the disposition of her child was broached. Nevertheless her smiling mask betrayed no trace to the American agents of the anguished turmoil within. Indeed her amiability aroused indignant and disgusted comment, and she was pronounced a soulless butterfly. This diagnosis of the woman was to be rudely shattered, when, beguiled by her seeming indifference, they relaxed somewhat of their vigilant espionage of her, and awoke one morning to find that the butterfly had flown beyond their reach.

The road of the mendicant, hunger, cold, and even shame were nearer to the gates of Nirvanna than life in splendour without her child. That was all part of the story of Madame Many Smiles.

History, in a measure, was to repeat itself in the life of Sunny. She had come to depend for her happiness upon her friends, and the shock of their impending departure was almost more than she could bear.

She spent many hours kneeling before Kuonnon, the Goddess of Mercy, throwing her petitions upon the lap of the goddess, and bruising her brow at the stone feet. It is sad to relate of Sunny, who so avidly had embraced the Christian faith, and was to the proud Mr. Sutherland an example of his labours in Japan, that in the hour of her great trouble she should turn to a heathen goddess. Yet here was Sunny, bumping her head at the stone feet. What could the Three-in-one God of the Reverend Mr. Sutherland do for her now? Sunny had never seen his face; but she knew well the benevolent comprehending smile of the Goddess of Mercy, and in Her, Sunny placed her trust. And so:

"Oh, divine Kuonnon, lovely Lady of Mercy, hear my petition. Do not permit my friends to leave Japan. Paralyse their feet. Blind their eyes that they may not see the way. Pray you close up the west ocean, so no ships may take my friends across. Hold them magnetised to the honourable earth of Japan."

Sitting back on her heels, having voiced her petition anxiously she scanned the face of the lady above her. The candles flickered and wavered in the soft wind, and the incense curled in a spiral cloud and wound in rings about the head of the celestial one. Sunny held her two hands out pleadingly toward the unmoving face.

"Lovely Kuonnon, it is true that I have tried magic to keep my friends with me, but even the oni (goblins) do not hear me, and my friends' boxes stand now in the ozashiki and the cruel carts carry them through the streets."

Her voice rose breathlessly, and she leaned up and stared with wide eyes at the still face above her, with its everlasting smile, and its lips that never moved.

"It is true! It is true!" cried Sunny excitedly. "The mission sir is right. There is no living heart in your breast. You are only stone. You cannot even hear my prayer. How then will you answer it?"

Half appalled by her own blasphemy, she shivered away from the goddess, casting terrified glances about her, and still sobbing in this gasping way, Sunny covered her face with her sleeve, and wended her way from the shrine to her home.

Here the dishevelled upset of the house brought home to her the unalterable fact of their certain going. Restraint and gloom had been in the once so jolly house, ever since Professor Barrowes had announced the time of departure. To the excited imagination of Sunny it seemed that her friends sought to avoid her. She could not understand that this was because they found it difficult to face the genuine suffering that their going caused their little friend. Sunny at the door of the living room sought fiercely to dissemble her grief. Never would she reveal uncouth and uncivilised tears; yet the smile she forced to her face now was more tragic than tears.

Jinx was alone in the room. The fat young man was in an especially gloomy and melancholy mood. He was wracking his brain for some solution to the problem of Sunny. To him, Sunny went directly, seating herself on the floor in front of him, so that he was obliged to look at the imploring young face, and had much ado to control the lump that would rise in Jinx's remorseful throat.

"Jinx," said Sunny persuasively, "I do not like to stay ad this Japan all alone also. I lig' you stay wiz me. Pray you do so, Mr. dear Jinx!"

"Gosh! I only wish I could, Sunny," groaned Jinx, sick with sympathy, "but, I can't do it. It's impossible. I'm not—not my own master yet. I did the best I could for you—wrote home and asked my folks if—if I could bring you along. Doggone them, anyway, they've kept the wires hot ever since squalling for me to get back."

"They do nod lig' Japanese girl?" asked Sunny sadly.

"Gosh, what do they know about it? I do, anyway. I think you're a peachy kid, Sunny. You suit me down to the ground, I'll tell the world, and you look-a-here, I'm coming back to see you, d'ye understand? I give you my solemn word I will."

"Jinx," said Sunny, without a touch of hope in her voice, "my father are say same thing; but—he never come bag no more."

Monty and Bobs, their arms loaded with sundry boxes of sweets and pretty things that aforetime would have charmed Sunny, came in from the street just then, and with affected cheer laid their gifts enticingly before the unbeguiled Sunny.

"See here, kiddy. Isn't this pretty!"

Bobs was swinging a long chain of bright red and green beads. Not so long before Sunny had led Bobs to that same string of beads, which adorned the counter of a dealer in Japanese jewelry, and had expressed to him her ambition to possess so marvellous a treasure. Bobs would have bought the ornament then and there; but it so happened that his finances were at their lowest ebb, his investment in the Syndicate having made a heavy inroad into the funds of the by no means affluent Bobs. The wherewithal to purchase the beads on the eve of departure had in fact come from some obscure corner of his resources, and he now dangled them enticingly before the girl's cold eyes. She turned a shoulder expressive of aversion toward the chain.

"I do nod lig' those kind beads," declared Sunny bitterly. Then upon an impulse, she removed herself from her place before Jinx, and kneeled in turn before Bobs, concentrating her full look of appeal upon that palpably moved individual.

"Mr. sir—Bobs, I do nod lig' to stay ad Japan, wizout you stay also. Please you take me ad America wiz you. I are not afraid those west oceans. I lig' those water. It is very sad for me ad Japan. I do nod lig' Japan. She is not Clistian country. Very bad people live on Japan. I lig' go ad America. Please you take me wiz you to-day."

Monty, hovering behind Bobs, was scowling through his bone-ribbed glasses. Through his seventeen-year-old brain raced wild schemes of smuggling Sunny aboard the vessel; of choking the watchful professor; of penning defiant epistles to the home folks; of finding employment in Japan and remaining firmly on these shores to take care of poor little Sunny. The propitiating words of Bobs appeared to Monty the sheerest drivel, untrue slush that it was an outrage to hand to a girl who trusted and believed.

Bobs was explaining that he was the beggar of the party. When he returned to America, he would have to get out and scuffle for a living, for his parents were not rich, and it was only through considerable sacrifice, and Bobs' own efforts at work (he had worked his way through college, he told Sunny) that he was able to be one of the party of students who following their senior year at college were travelling for a year prior to settling down at their respective careers. Bobs was too chivalrous to mention to Sunny the fact that his contribution to the Sunny Syndicate had caused such a shrinkage in his funds that it would take many months of hard work to make up the deficit; nor that he had even become indebted to the affluent Jinx in Sunny's behalf. What he did explain was the fact that he expected soon after he reached America, to land a job of a kind—he was to do newspaper work—and just as soon as ever he could afford it, he promised to send for Sunny, who was more than welcome to share whatever two-by-four home Bobs may have acquired by that time.

Sunny heard and understood little enough of his explanation. All she comprehended was that her request had been denied. Her own father's defective promises had made her forever sceptical of those of any other man in the world. Jinx in morose silence pulled fiercely on his pipe, brooding over the ill luck that dogged a fellow who was fat as a movie comedian and was related to an army of fat-heads who had the power to order him to come and go at their will. Jinx thought vengefully and ominously of his impending freedom. He would be of age in three months. Into his own hands then, triumphantly gloated Jinx, would fall the fortune of the house of Crawford, and *then* his folks would see! He'd show 'em! And as for Sunny—well, Jinx was going to demonstrate to that little girl what a man of his word was capable of doing.

Sunny, having left Bobs, was giving her full attention to Monty, who showed signs of panic.

"Monty, I wan' go wiz you ad America. *Please* take me there wiz you. I nod make no trobble for you. I be bes' nize girl you ever goin' see those worl. Please take me, Monty."

"Aw—all right, I will. You bet your life I will. That's settled, and you can count on me. *I'm* not afraid of *my* folks, if the other fellows are of theirs. I can do as I choose. I'll rustle up the money somehow. There's always a way, and they can say what they like at home, I intend to do things in my own way. My governor's threatening to cut me off; all the fellows' parents are—they're in league together, I believe, but I'm going to teach them all a lesson. I'll not stir a foot from Japan without you, Sunny. You can put that in your pipe and swallow it. *I* mean every last word *I* say."

"Now, now, now—not so hasty, young man, not so hasty! Not so free with promises you are unable to fulfil. Less words! Less words! More deeds!"

Professor Barrowes, pausing on the threshold, had allowed the junior member of the party he was piloting through Japan to finish his fiery tirade. He hung up his helmet, removed his rubbers, and rubbing his chilled hands to bring back the departed warmth, came into the room and laid the mail upon the table.

"Here you are, gentlemen. American mail. Help yourselves. All right, all right. Now, if agreeable, I desire to have a talk alone with Miss Sunny. If you young gentlemen will proceed with the rest of your preparations I daresay we will be on time. That will do, Goto. That baggage goes with us. Loose stuff for the steamer. Clear out."

Sunny, alone with the professor, made her last appeal.

"Kind Mr. Professor, please do not leave me ad those Japan. I wan go ad America wiz you. Please you permit me go also."

Professor Barrowes leaned over, held out both his hands, and as the girl came with a sob to him, he took her gently into his arms. She buried her face on the shabby coat of the old professor who had been such a good friend to her, and who with all his eccentricities had been so curiously loveable and approachable. After she had cried a bit against the old coat, Sunny sat back on her heels again, her two hands resting on the professor's knees and covered with one of his.

"Sunny, poor child, I know how hard it is for you; but we are doing the best we can. I want you to try and resign yourself to what is after all inevitable. I have arranged for you to go to the Sutherlands' home. You know them both—good people, Sunny, good people, in spite of their pious noise. Mr. Blumenthal has charge of your financial matters. You are amply provided for, thanks to the generosity of your friends, and I may say we have done everything in our power to properly protect you. You are going to show your appreciation by—er—being a good girl. Keep at your studies. Heed the instructions of Mr. Sutherland. He has your good at heart. I will not question his methods. We all have our peculiarities and beliefs. The training will do you no harm—possibly do you much good. I wish you always to remember that my interest in your welfare will continue, and it will be a pleasure to learn of your progress. When you can do so, I want you to write a letter to me, and tell me all about yourself."

"Mr. Professor, if I study mos' hard, mebbe I grow up to be American girl—jos same as her?"

Sunny put the question with touching earnestness.

"We-el, I am not prepared to offer the American girl as an ideal model for you to copy, my dear, but I take it you mean—er—that education will graft upon you our western civilisation, such as it is. It may do so. It may. I will not promise on that score. My mind is open. It has been done, no doubt. Many girls of your race have—ah—assimilated our own peculiar civilisation—or a veneer of the same. You are yourself mainly of white blood. Yes, yes, it is possible—quite probable in fact, that if you set out to acquire western ways, you will succeed in making yourself—er—like the people you desire to copy."

"And suppose I grow up lig' civilised girl, *then* I may live ad America?"

"Nothing to prevent you, my dear. Nothing to prevent you. It's a free country. Open to all. You will find us your friends, happy—I may say—overjoyed to see you again."

For the first time since she had learned the news of their impending departure a faint smile lighted up the girl's sad face.

"I stay ad Japan till I get—civil—ise."

She stood up, and for a moment looked down in mournful farewell on the seamed face of her friend. Her soft voice dropped to a caress.

"Sayonara, *mos* kindes' man ad Japan. I goin' to ask all those million gods be good to you."

And Professor Barrowes did not even chide her for her reference to the gods. He sat glaring alone in the empty room, fiercely rubbing his glasses, and rehearsing some extremely cutting and sarcastic phrases which he proposed to pen or speak to certain parents across the water, whose low minds suspected mud even upon a lily. His muttering reverie was broken by the quiet voice of Jerry. He had come out of the big window seat, where he had been all of the afternoon, unnoticed by the others.

"Professor Barrowes," said Jerry Hammond, "if you have no objection, I would like to take Sunny back with me to America."

Professor Barrowes scowled up at his favourite pupil.

"I do object, I do object. Emphatically. Most emphatically. I do not propose to allow you, or any of the young gentlemen entrusted to my charge, to commit an act that may be of the gravest consequences to your future careers."

"In my case, you need feel under no obligations to my parents. I am of age as you know, and as you also know, I purpose to go my own way upon returning home. My father asked me to wait till after this vacation before definitely deciding upon my future. Well, I've waited, and I'm more than ever determined not to go into the shops. I've a bit of money of my own—enough to give me a start, and I purpose to follow out my own ideas. Now as to Sunny. I found that kid. She's my own, when it comes down to that. I practically adopted her, and I'll be hanged if I'm going to desert her, just because my father and mother have some false ideas as to the situation."

"Leaving out your parents from consideration, I am informed that an engagement exists between you and a Miss—ah—Falconer, I believe the name is, daughter of your father's partner, I understand."

"What difference does that make?" demanded Jerry, setting his chin stubbornly.

"Can it be possible that you know human nature so little then, that you do not appreciate the feelings your fiancée is apt to feel toward any young woman you choose to adopt?"

"Why, Sunny's nothing but a child. It's absurd to refer to her as a woman, and if Miss Falconer broke with me for a little thing like that, I'd take my medicine I suppose."

"You are prepared, then, to break an engagement that has the most hearty approval of your parents, because of a quixotic impulse toward one you say is a child, but, young man, I would have you reflect upon the consequences to the child. Your kindness would act as a boomerang upon Sunny."

"What in the world do you mean?"

"I mean that Sunny is emphatically not a child. She was fifteen years old the other day. That is an exceedingly delicate period in a girl's life. We must leave the bloom upon the rose. It is a sensitive period in the life of a girl."

A long silence, and then Jerry:

"Right-oh! It's good-bye to Sunny!"

He turned on his heel and strode out to the hall. Professor Barrowes heard him calling to the girl upstairs in the cheeriest tone.

"Hi! up there, Sunny! Come on down, you little rascal. Aren't you going to say bye-bye to your best friend?"

Sunny came slowly down the stairs. At the foot, in the shadows of the hall she looked up at Jerry.

"Now remember," he rattled along with assumed merriment, "that when next we meet I expect you to be the Empress of Japan."

"Jerry," said Sunny, in a very little voice, her small eerie face seeming to shine with some light, as she looked steadily at him, "I lig' ask you one liddle bit favour before you go way from these Japan."

"Go to it. What is it, Sunny. Ask, and thou shalt receive."

Sunny put one hand on either of Jerry's arms, and her touch had a curiously electrical effect upon him. In the pause that ensued he found himself unable to remove his fascinated gaze from her face.

"Jerry, I wan' ask you, will you please give me those American—kiss—good-a-bye."

A great wave of tingling emotions swept over Jerry, blinding him to everything in the world but that shining face so close to his own. Sunny a child! Her age terrified him. He drew back, laughing huskily. He hardly knew himself what it was he was saying:

"I don't want to, Sunny—I don't——"

He broke away abruptly and, turning, rushed into the living room, seized his coat and hat, and was out of the house in a flash.

Professor Barrowes stared at the door through which Jerry had made his hurried exit. To his surprise, he heard Sunny in the hall, laughing softly, strangely. To his puzzled query as to why she laughed, she said softly:

"Jerry are afraid of me!"

And Professor Barrowes, student of human nature as he prided himself upon being, did not know that Sunny had stepped suddenly across the gap that separates a girl from a woman, and had come into her full stature.

CHAPTER VI

Time and environment work miracles. It is interesting to study the phases of emotion that one passes through as he emerges from youth into manhood. The exaggerated expressions, the unalterable conclusions, the tragic imaginings, the resolves, which he feels nothing can shake, how sadly and ludicrously and with what swiftness are they dissipated.

It came to pass that Sunny's friends across the sea reached a period where they thought of her vaguely only as a charming and amusing episode of an idyllic summer in the Land of the Rising Sun. Into the oblivion of the years, farther and farther retreated the face of the Sunny whose April smile and ingenuous ways and lovely face had once so warmed and charmed their young hearts.

New faces, new scenes, new loves, work and the claims and habits that fasten upon one with the years—these were the forces that engrossed them. I will not say that she was altogether forgotten in the new life, but at least she occupied but a tiny niche in their sentimental recollections. There were times, when a reference to Japan would call forth a murmur of pleasureable reminiscences, and humorous references to some remembered fantastic trick or trait peculiar to the girl, as:

"Do you remember when Sunny tried to catch that nightingale by putting salt near a place where she thought his tail might rest? I had told her she could catch him by putting salt on his tail, and the poor kid took me literally."

Jinx chuckled tenderly over the memory. In the first year after his return to America Jinx had borne his little friend quite often in mind, and had sent her several gifts, all of which were gratefully acknowledged by the Reverend Simon Sutherland.

"Will you ever forget" (from Bobs) "her intense admiration for Monty's white skin? She sat on the bank of the pool for nearly an hour, with the unfortunate kid under water, waiting for her to go away, while she waited for him to come out, because she said she wanted to see what a white body looked like 'wiz nothing but skin on for clothes.' I had to drag her off by main force. Ha, ha! I'll never forget her indignation, or her question whether Monty was 'ashamed his body.' The public baths of Nagasaki, you know, were social meeting places, and introductions under or above water quite the rule."

"I suppose," said Jerry, pulling at his pipe thoughtfully, "we never will get the Japanese point of view anent the question of morals."

"It's the shape of their eyes. They see things slant-wise," suggested Jinx brilliantly.

"But Sunny's eyes, as I recall them," protested Bobs, "were not slanting, and she had their point of view. You'll recall how the Proff had much ado to prevent her taking her own quaint bath in our 'lake' in beauty unadorned."

A burst of laughter broke forth here.

"Did he now? He never told me anything about that."

"Didn't tell me either, but I *heard* him. He explained to Sunny in the most fatherly way the whole question of morals from the day of Adam down, and she got him so tangled up and ashamed of himself that he didn't know where he was at. However, as I recall it, he must have won out in the contention, for you'll recall how she voiced such scathing and contemptuous criticism later on the public bathers of Japan, whom she said were 'igrant and nod god nize Americazan manner and wear dress cover hees body ad those bath.'"

"Ah, Sunny was a darling kid, take it from me. Just as innocent and sweet as a new-born babe." This was Jinx's sentimental contribution, and no voice arose to question his verdict.

So it will be perceived that her friends, upon the rare occasions when she was recalled to memory, still held her in loving, if humorous regard, and it was the custom of Jerry to end the reminiscences of Sunny with a big sigh and a dumping of the ash from his pipe, as he dismissed the subject with:

"Well, well, I suppose she's the Empress of Japan by now."

All of them were occupied with the concerns and careers that were of paramount importance to them. Monty, though but in his twenty-first year, an Intern at Bellevue; Bobs, star reporter on the *Comet*; Jinx, overwhelmingly rich, the melancholy and unwilling magnet of all aspiring mothers-in-law; Jerry, an outlaw from the house of Hammond, though his engagement to Miss Falconer bade fair to reinstate him in his parents' affections. He was doggedly following that star of which he had once told Sunny. Eight hours per day in an architect's office, and four or six hours in his own studio, was the sum of the work of Jerry. He "lived in the clouds," according to his people; but all the great deeds of the world, and all of the masterpieces penned or painted by the hand of man, Jerry knew were the creations of dreamers—the "cloud livers." So he took no umbrage at the taunt, and kept on reaching after what he had once told Sunny was that Jade of fortune—Beauty.

Somewhere up the State, Professor Barrowes pursued the uneven tenor of his way as Professor of Archeology and Zoology in a small college. Impetuous and erratic, becoming more restless with the years, he escaped the irritations and demands of the class room at beautiful intervals, when he indulged in a passion of research that took him into the far corners of the world, to burrow into the earth in search of things belonging to the remote dead and which he held of more interest than mere living beings. His fortunes were always uncertain, because of this eccentric weakness, and often upon returning from some such quest his friends had much ado to secure him a berth that would serve as an immediate livelihood. Such position secured, after considerable wire pulling on the part of Jerry and other friends, Professor Barrowes would be no sooner seated in the desired chair, when he would begin to lay plans for another escape. An intimate friendship existed between Jerry and his old master, and it was to Jerry that he invariably went upon his return from his archeological quests. Despite the difference in their years, there was a true kinship between these two. Each comprehended the other's aspirations, and in a way the passion for exploration and the passion for beauty is analogous. Jerry's parents looked askance at this friendship, and were accustomed to blame the Professor for their son's vagaries, believing that he aided and abetted and encouraged Jerry, which was true enough.

Of all Sunny's friends, Professor Barrowes, alone, kept up an irregular communication with the Sutherlands. Gratifying reports of the progress of their protégé came from the missionary at such times. Long since, it had been settled that Sunny should be trained to become a shining example to her race—if, in fact, the Japanese might be termed her race. It was the ambition of the good missionary to so instruct the girl that she would be competent to step into the missionary work, and with her knowledge of the Japanese tongue and ways, her instructor felt assured they could expect marvels from her in the matter of converting the heathen.

It is true the thought of that vivid little personality in the grey rôle of a preacher, brought somewhat wry faces to her friends, and exclamations even of distaste.

"Gosh!" groaned Jinx sadly, "I'd as lieves see her back on the tightrope."

"Imagine Sunny preaching! It would be a raving joke. I can just hear her twisting up her eight million gods and goddesses with our own deity," laughed Bobs.

"Like quenching a firefly's light, or the bruising of a butterfly's wings," murmured Jerry, dreamily, his head encircled with rings of smoke.

But then one becomes accustomed to even a fantastic thought. We accredit certain qualities and actions to individuals, and, in time, in our imaginations at least, they assume the traits with which we have invested them. After all, it was very comforting to think of that forlorn orphan child in the safe haven of a mission school.

So the years ran on and on, as they do in life, and as they do in stories such as this, and it came to pass, as written above, that Sunny disappeared into the fragrant corners of a pretty memory. There is where Sunny should perhaps have stayed, and thus my story come to a timely end.

Consider the situation. A girl, mainly of white blood, with just a drop of oriental blood in her—enough to make her a bit different from the average female of the species, enough, say, to give a snack of that savage element attributed to the benighted heathen. Rescued by men of her father's race from slavery and abuse; provided for for the rest of her days; under the instruction of a zealous and conscientious missionary and his wife, who earnestly taught her how to save the souls of the people of Japan. Sunny's fate was surely a desirable one, and as she progressed on the one side of the water, her friends on the other side were growing in sundry directions, ever outward and upward, acquiring new responsibilities, new loves, new claims, new passions with the passing of the years. What freak of fate therefore should interpose at this juncture, and thrust Sunny electrically into the lives of her friends again?

CHAPTER VII

On a certain bleak day in the month of March, J. Addison Hammond, Jr., tenaciously at work upon certain plans and drawings that were destined at a not far distant date to bring him a measure of fame and fortune, started impatiently from his seat and cursed that "gosh-ding-danged telephone."

Jerry at this stage of his picturesque career occupied what is known in New York City, and possibly other equally enlightened cities, as a duplex studio. Called "duplex" for no very clear reason. It consists of one very large room (called "atelier" by artistic tenants and those who have lived or wanted to live in France). This room is notable not merely for its size, but its height, the ceiling not unsimilar to the vaulted one of a church, or a glorified attic. Adjustable skylights lend the desired light. About this main room, and midway of the wall, is a gallery which runs on all four sides, and on this gallery are doors opening into sundry rooms designated as bedrooms. The arrangement is an excellent one, since it gives one practically two floors. That, no doubt, is why we call it "duplex." We have a weakness for one floor bungalows when we build houses these days, but for apartments and studios the epicure demands the duplex.

In this especial duplex studio there also abode one t, or as he was familiarly known to the friends of Jerry Hammond, "Hatty." Hatty, then, was the valet and man of all work in the employ of Jerry. He was a marvellous cook, an extraordinary house cleaner, an incomparable valet, and to complete the perfections of this jewel, possessed solely by the apparently fortunate Jerry, his manners, his face and his form were of that ideal sort seen only in fiction and never in life. Nevertheless the incomparable Hatton, or Hatty, was a visible fact in the life and studio of Jerry Hammond.

Having detailed the talents of Hatty, it is painful here to admit a flaw in the character of the otherwise perfect valet. This flaw he had very honestly divulged to Jerry at the time of entering his employ, and the understanding was that upon such occasions when said flaw was due to have its day, the master was to forbear from undue criticism or from discharging said Hatton from his employ. Hatton, at this time, earnestly assured the man in whose employ he desired to enter, that he could always depend upon his returning to service in a perfectly normal state, and life would resume its happy way under his competent direction.

It so happened upon this especial night, when that "pestiferous" telephone kept up its everlasting ringing—a night when Jerry hugged his head in his hands, calling profanely and imploringly upon Christian and heathen saints and gods to leave him undisturbed—that Hatton lay on his bed above, in a state of oblivion from which it would seem a charge of dynamite could not have awakened him.

For the fiftieth or possibly hundredth time Jerry bitterly swore that he would fire that "damned Englishman" (Hatton was English) on the following day. He had had enough of him. Whenever he especially needed quiet and service, that was the time the "damned Englishman" chose to break loose and go on one of his infernal sprees. For the fourth time within half an hour Jerry seized that telephone and shouted into the receiver:

"What in hades do you want?"

The response was a long and continuous buzzing, through which a jabbering female tongue screeched that it was Y. Dubaday talking. It sounded like "Y. Dubaday," but Jerry knew no one of that name, and so emphatically stated, adding to the fact that he didn't know anyone of that name and didn't want to, and if this was their idea of a joke———"

He hung up at this juncture, seized his head, groaned, walked up and down swearing softly and almost weeping with nervousness and distraction. Finally with a sigh of hopelessness as he realised the impossibility of concentrating on that night, Jerry gathered up his tools and pads, packed them into a portfolio, which he craftily hid under a mass of papers—Jerry knew where he could put his hands on any desired one—got his pipe, pulled up before the waning fire, gave it a shove, put on a fresh log, lit his pipe, stretched out his long legs, put his brown head back against the chair, and sought what comfort there might be left to an exasperated young aspirant for fame who had been interrupted a dozen times inside of an hour or so. Hardly had he settled down into this comparative comfort when that telephone rang again. Jerry was angry now—"hopping mad." He lifted that receiver with ominous gentleness, and his voice was silken.

"What can I do for you, fair one?"

Curiously enough the buzzing had completely stopped and the fair one's reply came vibrating clearly into his listening ear.

"Mr. Hammond?"

"Well, what of it?"

"Mr. Hammond, manager of some corporation or company in Japan?"

"What are you talking about?"

"If you'll hold the wire long enough to take a message from a friend I'll deliver it."

"Friend, eh? Who is he? I'd like to get a look at him this moment. Take your time."

"Well, I've no time to talk nonsense. This is the Y. W. C. A. speaking, and there's a young lady here, who says she—er—belongs to you. She———"

"What? Say that again, please."

"A young lady that appears to be related to you—says you are her guardian or manager or something of the sort. She was delivered to the Y. by the Reverend Miss Miriam Richardson, in whose care she was placed by the Mission Society of—er—Naggysack, Japan. One minute, I'll get her name again."

A photograph of Jerry at this stage would have revealed a young man sitting at a telephone desk, registering a conflict of feelings and emotions indicative of consternation, guilt, tenderness, fear, terror, compunction, meanness and idiocy. When that official voice came over the wire a second time, Jerry all but collapsed against the table, holding the receiver uncertainly in the direction of that ear that still heard the incredible news and confirmed his fears:

"Name—Miss Sindicutt."

Silence, during which the other end apparently heard not that exclamation of desperation: "Ye gods and little fishes!" for it resumed complacently:

"Shall we send her up to you?"

"No, no, for heaven's sake don't. That is, wait a bit, will you? Give me a chance to get over the———" Jerry was about to say "shock," but stopped himself in time and with as much composure as he could muster he told the Y. W. C. A. that he was busy just now, but would call later, and advise them what to do in the—under his breath he said "appalling"— circumstances.

Slowly Jerry put the receiver back on the hook. He remained in the chair like one who has received a galvanic shock. That Japanese girl, of a preposterous dream, had actually followed him to America! She was here— right in New York City. It was fantastic, impossible! Ha, ha! it would be funny, if it were not so danged impossible. In the United States, of all places! She, who ought to be right among her heathens, making good converts. What in the name of common sense had she come to the States

- 47 -

for? Why couldn't she let Jerry alone, when he was up to his neck in plans that he fairly knew were going to create an upheaval in the architectural world? Just because he had befriended her in his infernal youth, he could not be expected to be responsible for her for the rest of her days. Besides, he, Jerry, was not the only one in that comic opera Syndicate. The thought of his partners in crime, as they now seemed to him, brought him up again before that telephone, seizing upon it this time as a last straw.

He was fortunate to get in touch with all three of the members of the former Sunny Syndicate Limited. While Monty and Bobs rushed over immediately, Jinx escaped from the Appawamis Golf Club where for weeks he had been vainly trying to get rid of some of his superfluous flesh by chasing little red balls over the still snow bound course, flung himself into his powerful Rolls Royce, and went speeding along the Boston Post Road at a rate that caused an alarm to be sent out for him from point to point. Not swift enough, however, to keep up with the fat man in the massive car that "made the grade" to New York inside of an hour, and rushed like a juggernaut over the slick roads and the asphalt pavements of Manhattan.

Jerry's summons to his college friends had been in the nature of an S. O. S. call for help. On the telephone he vouchsafed merely the information that it was "a deadly matter of life and death."

The astounding news he flung like a bomb at each hastily arriving member of the late Syndicate. When the first excitement had subsided, the paramount feeling was one of consternation and alarm.

"Gosh!" groaned Jinx, "what in the name of thunderation are you going to do with a Japanese girl in New York City? I pity you, Jerry, for of course you are mainly responsible———"

"Responsible nothing———" from the indignant Jerry, wheeling about with a threatening look at that big "fathead." "I presume I was the *only* member of that—er—syndicate."

"At least it was your idea," said Monty, extremely anxious to get back to the hospital, where he had been personally supervising a case of Circocele.

"You might have known," suggested Bobs, "that she was bound to turn out a Frankenstein. Of course, we'll all stand by you, old scout, but you know how I am personally situated."

Jerry's wrathful glare embraced the circle of his renegade friends.

"You're a fine bunch of snobs. I'm not stuck myself on having a Jap girl foisted on to my hands, and there'll be a mess of explanations to my friends and people, and the Lord only knows how I'll ever be able to put my mind back on my work and——— At the same time, I'm not so white livered that I'm going to flunk the responsibility. We encouraged—invited her to join us out here. I did. You did, so did you, and you! I heard you all—every last one of you, and you can't deny it."

"Well, it was one thing to sentimentalise over a pretty little Jap in Japan," growled Bobs, who was not a snob, but in spite of his profession at heart something of a stickler for the conventions, "but it's another proposition here. Of course, as I said, we fellows all intend to stand by you." (Grunts of unwilling assent from Monty and Jinx.) "We aren't going to welch on our part of the job, and right here we may as well plan out some scheme to work this thing properly. Suppose we make the most of the matter for the present. We'll keep her down there at that 'Y.' Do you see? Then, we can each do something to—er—make it—well uncomfortable for her here. We'll freeze her out if it comes down to that. Make her feel that this U. S. A. isn't all it's cracked up to be, and she'll get home-sick for her gods and goddesses and at the psychological moment when she's feeling her worst, why we'll just slip her aboard ship, and there you are."

"Great mind! Marvellous intellect you got, Bobs. In the first place, the 'Y' informed me on the 'phone that they are sending her here. They are waiting now for me to give the word when to despatch her, in fact. Now the question is"—Jerry looked sternly at his friends—"which one of your families would be decent enough to give a temporary home to Sunny? My folks as you know are out of the reckoning, as I'm an outlaw from there myself."

Followed a heated argument and explanations. Monty's people lived in Philadelphia. He himself abode at the Bellevue Hospital. That, so he said, let him out. Not at all, from Jerry's point of view. Philadelphia, said Jerry, was only a stone's throw from New York. Monty, exasperated, retorted that he didn't propose to throw stones at his folks. Monty, who had made such warm promises to Sunny!

Bobs shared a five-room bachelor flat with two other newspaper men. Their hours were uncertain, and their actions erratic. Often they played poker till the small hours of the morning. Sunny would not fit into the atmosphere of smoke and disorder, though she was welcome to come, if she could stand the "gaff." Bobs' people lived in Virginia. His several sisters, Bobs was amusedly assured, would hardly put the girl from Japan at her ease.

Jinx, on whom Jerry now pinned a hopeful eye, blustered shamelessly, as he tried to explain his uncomfortable position in the world. When not at his club in New York, he lived with a sister, Mrs. Vanderlump, and her growing family in the Crawford mansion at Newport. Said sister dominated this palatial abode and brother Jinx escaped to New York upon occasions in a true Jiggsian manner, using craft and ingenuity always to escape the vigilant eye and flaying tongue of a sister who looked for the worst and found it. It was hard for Jinx to admit to his friends that he was horribly henpecked, but he appealed to them as follows:

"Have a heart about this thing. I ask you, what is a fellow to do when he's got a sister on his back like that? If she suspects every little innocent chorus girl of the town, what is she going to say to Sunny when that kid goes up before her in tights?"

It is extraordinary how we think of people we have not seen in years as they were when first we saw them. In the heat of argument, no one troubled to point out to Jinx that the Sunny who had come upon the tight rope that first night must have long since graduated from that reprehensible type of dress or rather undress.

Finally, and as a last resort, a night letter was despatched to Professor Timothy Barrowes. All were now agreed that he was the one most competent to settle the matter of the disposition of Sunny, and all agreed to abide by his decision.

At this juncture, and when a sense of satisfaction in having "passed the buck" to the competent man of archæology had temporarily cheered them, a tapping was heard upon the studio door. Not the thumping of the goblin's head of the Italian iron knocker; not the shriek of the electric buzzer from the desk below, warning of the approach of a visitor. Just a soft taptapping upon the door, repeated several times, as no one answered, and increasing in noise and persistence.

A long, a silent, a deadly pause ensued. At that moment each found himself attributing to that girl they had known in Japan, and whom they realised was on the other side of that door, certain characteristic traits and peculiarities charming enough in Japan but impossible to think of as in America. To each young man there came a mental picture of a bizarre and curious little figure, adorned with blazingly bright kimona and obi—a brilliant patch of colour, her bobbed hair and straight bangs seeming somehow incongruous and adding to her fantastic appearance. After all, in spite of her hair, she was typical of that land of crooked streets, and paper houses, and people who walked on the wrong side and mounted their horses from the front. The thought of that girl in New York City grated against their sensibilities. She didn't belong and she never could belong was their internal verdict.

It may have been only a coincidence, but it seemed weird, that Hatton, lately so dead to the world, should appear at that psychological moment on the steps of the gallery, immaculate in dress and with that cool air of superiority and efficiency that was part of his assets, descend in his stately and perfect way, approach the door as a butler should, and softly, imperturbably fling that door open. His back retained its stiff straight line, that went so well with the uniform Hatton insisted upon donning, but his head went sideways forward in that inimitable bow that Hatton always reserved for anything especially attractive in the female line.

Upon the threshold there looked back at Hatton, and then beyond him, a girl whom the startled young men took at first to be a perfect stranger. She wore a plain blue serge suit, belted at the waist, with a white collar and jabot. A sailor hat, slightly rolled, crushed down the hair that still shone above the face whose remarkable beauty owed much to a certain quaintness of expression. She stood silently, without moving, for what seemed a long moment to them all, and then suddenly she spoke, breathlessly and with that little catch in her voice, and her tone, her look, her words, her quick motions so characteristic of the little girl they had known, broke the spell of silence and let loose a flood of such warm memories that all the mean and harsh and contemptible thoughts of but a moment since were dissipated forever.

They crowded about her, hanging upon and hungry for her unabashed and delighted words, and dazzled by the girl's uncanny loveliness.

"Jinx! Thad are you! I know you by your so nize fat!"

She had not lost her adorable accent. Indeed, if they could but have realised it, Sunny had changed not at all. She had simply grown up.

Jinx's soft hands were holding the two little fragrant ones thrust so joyously into his own. The fat fellow fought a sudden maddening desire to hug like a bear the girl whose bright eyes were searching his own so lovingly.

"Monty! Oh, you have grow into whole mans. *How* it is nize. And you still smile on me troo those glass ad you eye."

Smile! Monty was grinning like the proverbial Cheshire cat. That case of Circocele at Bellevue hospital had vanished into the dim regions of young Monty's mind. Anyway there were a score of other Internes there, and Monty had his permit in his pocket.

"Bobs! Is thad youself, wiz those fonny liddle hair grow om your mout'. *How* it is grow nize on you face. I lig' him there."

Any doubt that Bobs had experienced as to the desirability of that incipient moustache vanished then and there.

And Jerry! Jerry, for the last, to be looked at with shining eyes, till something tightened in his throat, and his mind leaped over the years and felt again that dizzy, tingling, electrical sensation when Sunny had asked him to kiss her.

CHAPTER VIII

That "even tenor of their ways," to which reference has already been made, ceased indeed to bear a remote resemblance to evenness. It may be recorded here, that for one of them at least, Sunny's coming meant the hasty despatch of his peace of mind. Their well laid schemes to be rid of her seemed now in the face of their actions like absurd aberrations that they were heartily ashamed of.

It is astonishing how we are affected by mere clothes. Perhaps if Sunny had appeared at the door of Jerry Hammond's studio arrayed in the shining garments of a Japanese, some measure of their alarm might have remained. But she came to their door as an American girl. That Sunny should have stood the test of American clothes, that she shone in them with a distinction and grace that was all her own, was a matter of extreme pride and delight to her infatuated friends. Appearances play a great part in the imagination and thought of the young American. It was the fantastic conception they had formed of her, and the imagined effect of her strange appearance in America that had filled them with misgiving and alarm—the sneaky sort of apprehension one feels at being made conspicuous and ridiculous. There was an immense relief at the discovery that their fears were entirely unfounded. Sunny appeared a finished product in the art of dressing. Not that she was fashionably dressed. She simply had achieved the look of one who belonged. She was as natural in her clothes as any of their sisters or the girls they knew. There was this difference, however: Sunny was one of those rare beings of earth upon whom the Goddess of Beauty has ineffaceably laid her hands. Her loveliness, in fact, startled one with its rareness, its crystal delicacy. One looked at the girl's face, and caught his breath and turned to look again, with that pang of longing that is almost pain when we gaze upon a masterpiece.

Yet "under the skin" she was the same confiding, appealing, mischievous little Sunny who had pushed her way into the hearts of her friends.

Her mission in America, much as it aroused the mirth of her friends, was a very serious one, and it may be here stated, later, an eminently successful one. Sunny came as an emissary from the mission school to collect funds for the impoverished mission. Mr. Sutherland, a Scotchman by birth, was not without a canny and shrewd streak to his character, and he had not forgotten the generous contributions in the past of the rich young Americans whose protégé Sunny had been.

All this, however, does not concern the devastating effect of her presence in the studio of Jerry Hammond. There, in fact, Sunny had taken up an apparently permanent residence, settling down as a matter of course and right, and indeed assisted by the confused and alternately dazed and beguiled Jerry.

Her effects consisted of a bag so small, and containing but a few articles of Japanese silk clothing and a tiny gift for each of her dear friends. Indeed, the smallness of Sunny's luggage appealed instantly to her friends, who determined to purchase for her all the pretty clothes her heart should desire. This ambition to deck Sunny in the fine raiment of New York City was satisfactorily realised by each and everyone of the former Syndicate, Sunny accompanying them with alacrity, overjoyed by those delicious shopping tours, the results of which returned in Jinx's Rolls Royce, Monty's taxi, Bobs' messenger boys, and borne by hand by Jerry. These articles, however, became such a bone of contention among her friends, each desiring her to wear his especial choice, that Sunny had her hands full pleasing them all. She compromised by wearing a dress donated by Monty, hat from Jinx, a coat from Jerry, and stockings and gloves from Bobs. It was finally agreed by her friends that there should be a cessation to the buying of further clothes for Sunny. Instead an allowance of money was voted and quickly subscribed to by all, and after that, Sunny, with the fatherly aid of a surprisingly new Hatton, did her own purchasing.

Of her four friends, Jerry was possibly the happiest and the unhappiest at this time. He was a prey to both exhilaration and panic. He moved heaven and earth to make Sunny so comfortable and contented in his studio, that all thought of returning to Japan would be banished forever from her mind. On the other hand, he rushed off, panic stricken and sent telegrams to Professor Barrowes, entreating him to come at once and relieve Jerry of his dangerous charge. His telegrams, however, were unfruitful, for after an aggravating delay, during which Sunny became, like Hatton, one of the habits and necessities of Jerry's life, the Telegraph Company notified him that Professor Barrowes was no longer at that particular school of learning, and that his address there was unknown. Jerry, driven to extremities by the situation in his studio, made himself such a nuisance to the Telegraph Company, that they bestirred themselves finally and ascertained that the last address of Professor Timothy Barrowes was Red Deer, Alberta, Canada. Now Red Deer represented nothing to Jerry Hammond save a town in Canada where a wire would reach his friend. Accordingly he despatched the following:

  Professor Timothy Barrowes,
  Red Deer, Alberta, Canada.

Come at once. Sunny in New York. Need you take her charge. Delay dangerous. Waiting for you. Come at once. Answer at once. Important.

J. ADDISON HAMMOND.

Professor Barrowes received this frantic wire while sitting on a rock very close to the edge of a deep excavation that had recently been dug on the side of a cliff towering above a certain portion of the old Red Deer River. Below, on a plateau, a gang of men were digging and scraping and hammering at the cliff. Not in the manner of the husky workers of northwestern Canada, but carefully, tenderly. Not so carefully, however, but the tongue of the Professor on the rock above castigated and nagged and warned. Ever and anon Sunny's old friend would leap down into the excavation, and himself assist the work physically.

As stated, Jerry's telegram came to his hand while seated upon aforesaid rock, was opened, and absent-mindedly scanned by Jerry's dear friend, and then thrust hastily into the professor's vest pocket, there to remain for several days, when it accidentally was resurrected, and he most thoughtfully despatched a reply, as follows:

Jeremy Addison Hammond,
12 West 67th St.,
New York City, U. S. A.

Collect.

Glad to hear from you. Especially so this time. Discovered dinosaur antedating post pleocene days. Of opinion Red Deer district contains greatest number of fossils of antique period in world. Expect discoveries prove historical event archeological world. Will bring precious find New York about one month or six weeks. Need extra funds transportation dinosaur and guard for same. Expect trouble Canadian government in re-taking valuable find across border. Much envy and propaganda take credit from U. S. for most important discovery of century. Get in communication right parties New York, Washington if necessary. Have consul here wired give full protection and help. Information sent confidential. Do not want press to get word of remarkable find until fossil set up in museum. See curator about arrangements. May be quoted as estimating age as quaternary period. Wire two thousand dollars extra. Extraordinary find. Greatest moment my life. Note news arrival New York Sunny. Sorry unable be there take charge. Dinornis more important Sunny.

TIMOTHY BARROWES.

What Jerry said when he tore open and read that long expected telegram would not bear printing. Suffice it to say that his good old friend was consigned by the wrathful and disgusted Jerry to a warmer region than Mother Earth. Then, squaring his shoulders like a man, and setting his chin grimly, Jerry took up the burden of life, which in these latter days had assumed for him such bewildering proportions.

That she was an amazing, actual part of his daily life seemed to him incredible, and beguiling and fascinating as life now seemed to him with her, and wretched and uncertain as it was away from her, his alarm increased with every day and hour of her abode in his house. He assured himself repeatedly that there was no more harm in Sunny living in his apartment than there was in her living in his house in Japan. What enraged the befuddled Jerry at this time was the officious attitude of his friends. Monty took it upon himself to go room hunting for a place for Sunny, and talked a good deal about the results he expected from a letter written to Philadelphia. He did not refer to Sunny now as a stone. Monty was sure that the place for Sunny was right in that Philadelphia home, presided over by his doting parents and little brothers and sisters, and where it was quite accessible for week-end visits.

Jinx, after a stormy scene with his elder sister in which he endeavoured to force Sunny upon the indignant and suspicious Mrs. Vanderlump, left in high dudgeon the Newport home in which he had been born, and which was his own personal inheritance, and with threats never to speak to his sister again, he took up his residence at his club, just two blocks from the 67th Street studio.

Bobs cleared out two of his friends from the flat, bought some cretonne curtains with outrageous roses and patches of yellow, purple, red and green, hung these in dining room and bedroom and parlour, bought a brand new victrola and some quite gorgeous Chinese rugs, and had a woman in cleaning for nearly a week. To his friends' gibes and suggestions that he apparently contemplated matrimony, Bobs sentimentally rejoined that sooner or later a fellow got tired of the dingy life of a smoke-and-card-filled flat and wanted a bit of real sweetness to take away the curse of life. He acquired two lots somewhere on Long Island and spent considerable time consulting an architect, shamefully ignoring Jerry's gifts in that line.

That his friends, who had so savagely protested again sharing the burden of Sunny, should now try to go behind his back and take her away from him was in the opinion of Jerry a clue to the kind of characters they possessed, and of which hitherto he had no slightest suspicion.

Jerry, at this time, resembled the proverbial dog in the manger. He did not want Sunny himself—that is, he dared not want Sunny—but the thought of her going to any other place filled him with anguish and resentment. Nevertheless he realised the impossibility of maintaining her much longer in his studio. Already her presence there had excited gossip and speculation in the studio building, but in that careless and bohemian atmosphere with which denizens of the art world choose to surround themselves the lovely young stranger in the studio of Jerry Hammond aroused merely smiling and indulgent curiosity. Occasionally a crude joke or inquiry from a neighbouring artist aroused murder in the soul of the otherwise civilised Jerry. That anyone could imagine anything wrong with Sunny seemed to him beyond belief.

Not that he felt always kindly toward Sunny. She aroused his ire more often than she did his approval. She was altogether too free and unconventional, in the opinion of Jerry, and in a clumsy way he tried to teach her certain rules of deportment for a young woman living in the U. S. A. Sunny, however, was so innocent and so evidently earnest in her efforts to please him, that he invariably felt ashamed and accused himself of being a pig and a brute. Jerry was, indeed, like the unfortunate boatman, drifting toward the rocks, and seeing only the golden hair of the Lorelei.

Sunny had settled down so neatly and completely in his studio that it would have been hard to know how she was ever to be dislodged. Her satisfaction and delight and surprise at every object upon the place was a source of immense satisfaction and entertainment to Jerry. It should be mentioned here, that an unbelievable change could have been observed also in Hatton. The man was discovered to be human. His face cracked up in smiles that were real, and clucks that bore a remote resemblance to human laughter issued at intervals from the direction of the kitchen, whither he very often hastily departed, his hand over mouth, after some remark or action of Sunny that appeared to smite his funny bone.

The buttons on the wall were a never failing source of enchantment to Sunny. To go into her own room in the dark, brush her hand along the wall, touch an ivory button, and see the room spring into light charmed her beyond words. So, too, the black buttons that, pressed, caused bells to ring in the lower part of the house. But the speaking tube amazed and at first almost terrified her. Jerry sprang the works on her first. While in her room, a sudden screech coming from the wall, she looked panically about her, and then started back as a voice issued forth from that tube, hailing her by name. Spirits! Here in this so solid and material America! It was only after Jerry, getting no response to his calls of "Sunny! Hi! Sunny! Come on down! Come on down! Sunny! I want you!" ran up the stairs, knocked at her door and stood laughing at her in the doorway, that the colour came back to her cheeks. He was so delighted with the experiments, that he led her to the telephone and initiated her into that mystery. To watch Sunny's face, as with parted lips, and eyes darkened by excitement, she listened to the voice of Jinx, Monty or Bobs, and then suddenly broke loose and chattered sweet things back, was in the opinion of Jerry worth the price of a dozen telephones. However, he cut short her interviews with the delighted fellows at the other end, as he did not wish to have them impose on her good nature and take up too much of the girl's time.

The victrola and the player-piano worked day and night in Sunny's behalf, and it was not long before she could trill back some of the songs. Upon one occasion they pulled up the rugs, and Sunny had her first lesson in dancing. Jerry told her she took to dancing "like a duck does to water." He honestly believed he was doing a benevolent and worthy act in surrounding the young girl with his arms and moving across the floor with her to the music of the victrola. He would not for worlds have admitted to himself that as his arms encircled Sunny, Jerry felt just about as near to heaven as he ever hoped to get, though premonitions that all was not normal with him came hazily to his mind as he dimly realised that that tingling sensation that contact with Sunny created was symptomatic of the chaos within. However, dancing with Sunny, once she had acquired the step, which she, a professional dancer in Japan, sensed immediately, was sheer joy, and all would have been well, had not his friends arrived just when they were not wanted, and, of course, Sunny, the little fool, had instantly wanted to try her new accomplishment upon her admiring and too willing friends. The consequence was Jerry's evening was completely spoiled, and what he meant just as an innocent diversion was turned into a "riotous occasion" by a "bunch of roughnecks," who took advantage of a little innocent girl's eagerness to learn to dance, and handled her "a damn sight too familiarly" to suit the paternal—he considered it paternal—taste of Jerry.

Jerry, as Sunny passed in the arms of the light-footed Jinx, whose dancing was really an accomplishment, registered several vows. One was he proposed to give Sunny herself a good calling down. The other he purposed curtailing some of the visits of the gang, and putting a stop once and for all to the flow of gifts that were in his opinion rotten taste on the part of Jinx, a joke coming from Monty, plainly suffering a bad case of puppy love, and as for Bobs, no one knew better than Jerry did that he could ill afford to enter into a flower competition with Jinx. That Rolls Royce, when not bearing the enchanted Sunny through the parks and even on little expeditions into the byways and highways of the Great White Road, which runs through Westchester county, was parked not before Jinx's club, or the garage, but, with amazing impudence before the door of that duplex studio. Jerry intended to have a heart-to-heart talk with old Jinx on that score.

Even at home, Sunny had wrought havoc. Before she had been three days upon the place, Hatton, the stony faced and spare of tongue, had confided to her the whole history of his life, and explained how his missus had driven him to drink.

"It's 'ard on a man, miss. 'E tries to do 'is best in life, but it's 'ard, miss, when there's a woman 'as believes the worst, and brings out the worst in a man, miss, and man is only yuman, only yuman, miss, and all yuman beings 'as their failings, as no doubt you know, miss."

Sunny did know. She told Hatton that she was full of failings. She didn't think him a bad man at all because once in a long time he drank a little bit. Lots of men did that. There was the Count of Matsuyama. He had made many gifts to the Shiba temple, but he loved sake very much, and often in the tea-gardens the girls were kept up very late, because the Count of Matsuyama never returned home till he had drunk all the sake on the place, and that took many hours.

Gratuitously, and filled with a sudden noble purpose, Hatton gave Sunny his solemn promise never again to touch the inebriating cup. She clapped her hands with delight at this, and cried.

"Ho! How you are nicer man now. Mebbe you wife she come bag agin unto you. How thad will be happy for you."

"No, no, miss," sadly and hastily Hatton rejoined, "you see, miss, there was another woman in the case also, what the French call, miss: Shershy la Fam. I'm sorry, miss, but I'm only yuman, beggin' your pardon, miss."

Sunny had assumed many of the duties that were previously Hatton's. The kitchenette was her especial delight. Here swathed in a long pongee smock, her sleeves rolled up, Sunny concocted some of those delectable dishes which her friends named variously: Sunny Syndicate Cocktail; Puree al la Sunny; Potatoes au Sunny; Sweet pickles par la Sunny, and so forth. Her thrift also cut down Jerry's bills considerably, and he was really so proud of her abilities in this line that he gave a special dinner to which he generously invited all three of their mutual friends, and announced at the table that the meal was entirely concocted by Sunny at a price inconceivably low.

The piéce de resistance of this especial feast was a potato dish. Served in a casserole, it might at first sight have been taken for a glorified potatoes au gratin; but, no, when tasted it revealed its superior qualities. The flushed and pleased Sunny, sitting at the head of the table, and dishing out the third or fourth serving to her admiring friends, was induced to reveal to her friends of what the dish was composed. The revelation, it is regrettable to state, convulsed and disconcerted her friends so that they ceased to eat the previously much appreciated dish. Sunny proudly informed them that her dish was made up mainly of potato peelings, washed, minced and scrambled in a mess of odds and ends in the way of pieces of cheese, mushrooms, meat, and various vegetables garnered from plates of a recently wasteful meal.

Her explanation caused such a profound silence for a moment, which was followed by uneasy and then unrepressed mirth, that she was disconcerted and distressed. Her friends consoled her by telling her that it didn't matter what she made dishes of; everything she did was exactly right, which made it a bit harder to explain that the shining pan under the kitchen sink was the proper receptacle for all leftovers on the plates. She was reconciled completely moreover, when Jerry assured her that the janitor was kicking over the empty dinner pails that she had been sending down the dumbwaiter.

CHAPTER IX

Sunny had certain traits that contributed largely to what seemed almost an unconscious conspiracy to rob Jerry Hammond of his peace of mind. There was a resemblance in her nature to a kitten.

To maintain a proper decorum in his relations with his guest, Jerry was wont, when alone, to form the firm resolution to hold her at arm's length. This was far from being an easy matter. It was impossible for him to be in the room with Sunny and not sooner or later find her in touch with him. She had a habit of putting her hand into his. She slipped under his most rigid guard, and acquired a bad trick of pressing close to his side, and putting her arm through his. This was all very well when they took their long walks through the park or up and down Riverside Drive. She could not see the reason why if she could walk arm in arm with Jerry when they climbed on the top of one of the busses that rolled up the wonderful drive she should not continue linked with her friend. In fact, Sunny found it far more attractive and comfortable to drive arm in arm with Jerry than walk thus with him. For, when walking, she loved to rove off from the paths, to make acquaintance with the squirrels and the friendly dogs.

Her near proximity, however, had its most dangerous effect in the charmed evenings these two spent together, too often, however, marred by the persistent calls of their mutual friends. At these times, Sunny had an uncanny trick of coming up at the back of Jerry, when that unconscious young man by the fireplace was off in a day dream (in which, by the way, in a vague way, herself was always a part), and resting her cheek upon the brown comfortable head, there to stay till her warm presence startled him into wakefulness, and he would explode one of his usual expressions of these days:

"Don't do that, I say!"

"Keep your hands off me, will you?"

"Don't come so close."

"Keep off—keep off, I say."

"I don't like it."

"For heaven's sake, Sunny, will nothing teach you civilised ways?"

At these times Sunny always retired very meekly to a distant part of the room, where she would remain very still and crushed looking, and, shortly, Jerry, overcome with compunction, would coax her to a nearer proximity mentally and physically.

Another disturbing trick which Jerry never had had the heart to ban was that of kneeling directly in front of him, her two hands upon his own knees. From this vantage point, with her friendly expressive and so lovely face raised to his, she would naïvely pour out to him her innocent confidences. After all, he savagely argued within himself, what harm in the world was there in a little girl kneeling by your side, and even laying her head, if it came down to that, at times upon a fellow's knee? It took a rotten mind to discover anything wrong with that, in the opinion of Jerry Hammond.

However, there is a limit to all things, and that limit was reached on a certain evening in early spring, a dangerous season, as we all know. "If you give some people an inch they'll take a mile," Jerry at that time angrily muttered, the humour of the situation not at all appealing to him.

He was going over a publication on Spanish Architecture, Catalonian work of the 14th and 15th centuries. Sunny was enjoying herself very innocently at the piano player, and Jerry should, as he afterwards admitted to himself, have "left well enough alone." However it be, nothing would do but he must summon Sunny to his side to share the pleasure of looking at these splendid examples of the magnificent work of the great Spanish architect Fabre.

Now Sunny possessed, to an uncanny degree, that gift of understanding which is extremely rare with her sex. She possessed it, in fact, to such a fine degree, that nearly everyone who met her found himself pouring out the history of his life into her sympathetic and understanding little ear. There was something about her way of looking at one, a sort of hanging absorbedly upon one's narrative of their history, that assured the narrator that he not only had the understanding but the sympathy of his pretty listener.

Jerry, therefore, summoned her from her diversions at the piano-player, which she hastened to leave, though the record was her favourite, "Gluhwormchen." Her murmuring exclamations above his shoulder revealed her instant enthusiasm and appreciation of just those details that Jerry knew would escape the less artistic eye of an ordinary person. She held pages open, to prolong the pleasure of looking at certain window traceries; she picked out easily the Geometrical Gothic type, and wanted Jerry's full explanation as to its difference to those of another period. Her little pink forefinger ever found points of interest in the sketches which made him chuckle with delight and pride. The value of Sunny's criticism and opinion, moreover, was enhanced by the fact that she conveyed to the young man her conviction, that while of course these were incredibly marvellous examples of the skill of ancient Spanish architects, they were not a patch on the work which J. Addison Hammond was going to do in the not far distant future. Though he protested against this with proper modesty, he was nevertheless beguiled and bewitched by the shining dream she called up. He had failed to note that she was perched on the arm of his chair, and that her head rested perilously near to his own. Possibly he would never have discovered this at all had not an accident occurred that sent Hatton, busy on some task or other about the studio, scurrying in undignified flight from the room, with his stony face covered with his hands. From the kitchen regions thereafter came the sound of suppressed clucks, which by this time could have been recognised as Hatton's laughter.

What happened was this: At a moment when a turned leaf revealed a sketch of ravishing splendour, Sunny's breathless admiration, and Jerry's own motion of appreciation (one fist clapped into the palm of the other hand), caused Sunny to slip from the arm of the chair onto Jerry's knee.

Jerry arose. To do him justice, he arose instantly, depositing both book and Sunny upon the floor. He then proceeded to read her such a savage lecture upon her pagan ways, that the evident effect was so instantly apparent on her, that he stopped midway, glared, stared at the crushed little figure, so tenderly closing the upset book, and then turned on his heel and made an ignominious and undignified exit from the room.

"What's the use? What's the use?" demanded Jerry of the unresponsive walls. "Hang it all, this sort of thing has got to stop. What in Sam Hill is keeping that blamed Proff?"

He always liked to imagine at these times that his faith was pinned upon the early coming of Professor Barrowes, when he was assured the hectic state of affairs in his studio would be clarified and Sunny disposed of once and forever. Sunny, however, had been nearly a month now in his studio, and in spite of a hundred telegrams to Professor Barrowes, demanding to know the exact time of his arrival, threatening moreover to hold back that $2,000 required to bring the dashed Dinornis from Red Deer, Alberta, Canada, to New York City, U. S. A., he got no satisfactory response from his old-time teacher. That monomaniac merely replied with letter-long telegrams—very expensive coming from the extreme northwestern part of Canada to New York City, giving more detailed information about the above mentioned Dinornis, or Dynosaurus, or whatever he called it, and explaining why more and more funds were required. It seems the Professor was tangled up in quite a serious dispute with the Canadian authorities. Some indignant English residents of Canada had aroused the alarm of Canadians, by pointing out that Dynosaureses were worth as much as radium, and that a mere Yankee should not be permitted to carry off those fossilized bones of the original inhabitants of Canada, which ought, instead, to be donated to the noble English nation across the sea.

As Jerry paced his floor he paused to reread the words of the motto recently pinned upon his wall, and, of course, it was as follows: "Honi soit qui mal y pense." That was enough for Jerry. There was no question of the fact that he had been "a pig and a brute," terms often in these days applied by himself to himself. Sunny was certainly not to be blamed for the accident of slipping from the arm of his chair. True, he had already told her that she was not to sit on that arm, but that was a minor matter, and there was no occasion for his making a "mountain out of a molehill."

Having arrived at the conclusion that, as usual, he, not Sunny, was the one to blame, it was in the nature of Jerry that he should hurriedly descend to admit his fault. Downstairs, therefore again, and into the now empty studio. Sounds came from the direction of the kitchen that were entirely too sweet to belong to the "pie-faced" Hatton, whose disgusting recent mirth might mean the loss of his job, ominously thought Jerry.

In the kitchen Sunny was discovered on her knees with her lips close to a small hole in the floor in the corner of the room. She was half whistling, half whispering, and she was scattering something into and about that hole, which had been apparently cut out with a vegetable knife, that looked very much like cheese and breadcrumbs. Presently the amazed Jerry saw first one and then another tiny face appear at that hole, and there then issued forth a full-fledged family of the mouse species, young and old, large and small, male and female. The explanation of the previously inexplicable appearance in the studio of countless mice was now perfectly clear, and the guiltlessness of that accused janitor made visible. Jerry's ward had been feeding and cultivating mice! At his exclamation, she arose reproachfully, the mice scampering back into their hole.

"Oh!" said Sunny, regret, not guilt, visible on her face, "you are fright away my honourable mice, and thas hees time eat on hees dinner."

She put the rest of her crumbs into the hole, and called down coaxingly to her pets that breakfast would be ready next day.

"You mustn't feed mice, you little fool!" burst from Jerry. "They'll be all over the house. They are now. Everybody in the building's kicking about it."

"Honourable mice very good animals," said Sunny with conviction. "Mebbe some you and my ancestor are mice now. You kinnod tell 'bout those. Mice got very honourable history ad Japan. I am lig' them very much."

"That'll do. Don't say another word. I'll fix 'em. Hi! you, Hatton! Doggone you, you must have known about this."

"Very sorry, sir, but orders from you, sir, was to allow Miss Sunny to have her way in the kitchen, sir. 'Hi tries to obey you, sir, and 'hi 'adn't the 'eart to deprive Miss Sunny of her honly pets, sir. She's honly yuman, sir, and being alone 'hall day, so young, sir, 'as 'ankerings for hinnocent things to play with."

"That'll do, Hatton. Nail up that hole. Get busy."

Nevertheless, Hatton's words sunk into the soul of Jerry. To think that even the poor working man was kinder to little Sunny than was he! He ignored the fact that as Hatton nailed tin over the guilty hole his shoulders were observed to be shaking, and those spasmodic clucks emanated at intervals also from him. In fact, Hatton, in these days, had lost all his previously polished composure. That is to say, at inconvenient moments, he would burst into this uncontrollable clucking, as for instance, when waiting on table, observing a guest devouring some special edible concocted by Sunny, he retired precipitately from service at the table to the kitchen, to be discovered there by the irate Jerry, who had followed him, sitting on a chair with tears running down his cheeks. To the threatened kicking if he didn't get up and behave himself, Hatton returned:

"Oh, sir, hi ham honly yuman, and the gentleman was ravim' so about them 'spinnuges,' sir, has 'ees hafter calling them."

"Well, what are they then?" demanded Jerry.

"Them's weeds, sir," whispered Hatton wiping his eyes. "Miss Sunny, I seen her diggin' them up in the lot across the way, and she come up the fire escape with them in 'er petticoat, sir, and she 'ad four cats in the petticoat also, sir. She's feedin' arf the population of cats in this neighbourhood, sir."

Jerry had been only irritated at that time. He knew that Sunny's "weeds" were perfectly edible and far more toothsome in fact than mere spinach. Trust her Japanese knowledge to know what was what in the vegetable kingdom. However, mice were a more serious matter. There was an iron clad rule in the building that no live stock of any kind, neither dogs, cats, parrots, or birds or reptiles of any description, (babies included in the ban) were to be lodged on these de luxe premises. Still, as Jerry watched Sunny's brimming eyes, the eyes of one who sees her dear friends imprisoned and doomed to execution, while Hatton nailed the tin over the holes, he felt extremely mean and cruel.

"I'm awfully sorry, Sunny, old scout," he said, "but you know we can't possibly have *mice* on the place. Now if it were something like—like, well a dog, for instance———"

"I *are* got a nize dog," said Sunny, beginning to smile through her tears.

Apprehension instantly replaced the compunction on Jerry's face—apprehension that turned to genuine horror, however, when Sunny opened the window onto the fire escape, and showed him a large grocer's box, upholstered and padded with a red article that looked suspiciously like a Japanese petticoat. Digging under this padded silk, Sunny brought forth the yellowest, orneriest, scurviest and meanest-looking specimen of the dog family that it had ever been Jerry's misfortune to see. She caught this disreputable object to her breast, and nestled her darling little chin against the wriggling head, that persisted in ducking up to release a long red tongue that licked her face with whines of delight and appreciation.

"Sunny! For the love of Mike! Where in the name of all the pagan gods and goddesses of Japan did you get that god-forsaken mutt from? If you wanted a dog, why in Sam Hill didn't you tell me, and I'd have gotten you a regular dog—if they'd let me in the house."

"Jerry, he are a regular dog also. I buyed him from the butcher gentleman, who was mos' kind, and he charge me no moaney for those dog, bi-cause he are say he are poor mans, and those dog came off those street and eat him up those sausage. So that butcher gentleman he are sell him to me, and he are my own dog, and I are love my Itchy mos' bes' of all dogs."

And she hugged her little cur protectingly to her breast, her bright eyes with the defiant look of a little mother at bay.

"Itchy!"

"Thad are my dog's name. The butcher gentleman, he say he are scratch on his itch all those time, so I are name him Itchy. Also I are cure on those itch spot, for I are wash him every day, and now he are so clean he got only two flea left on his body."

"By what process of mathematics, will you tell me, did you arrive at the figure of two?" demanded the stunned young man, thrusting his two fists deep into his pocket and surveying Sunny and the aforesaid dog as one might curious specimens in the Bronx zoo.

"Two? Two flea?" Sunny passed her hand lovingly and sympathetically over her dog's yellow body, and replied so simply that even an extremely dense person would have been able to answer that arithmetic problem.

"He are scratch him in two place only."

Jerry threw back his head and burst into immoderate laughter. He laughed so hard that he was obliged to sit down on a chair, while Hatton on the floor sat down solidly also, and desisted with his hammering. Jerry's mirth having had full sway, hands in pocket he surveyed Sunny, as, lovingly, she returned her protesting cur to its silken retreat.

"Sunny! Sunny!" said Jerry, shaking his head. "You'll be the death of me yet."

Sunny regarded him earnestly at that.

"No, Jerry, do not say those. I are not want to make you death. Thas very sad—for die."

"What are we going to do about it? They'll never let you keep a dog here. Against the rules."

"No, no, it are no longer 'gainst those rule. I are speag wiz the janitor gentleman, and he are say: 'Thas all ride, seein' it's you!'"

"He did, did he? Got around him too, did you? You'll have the whole place demoralised if you keep on."

"I are also speag ad those landlord," confessed Sunny innocently, "bicause he are swear on those janitor gentleman, account someone ad these house are spik to him thad I are got dog. And thad landlord gentleman he come up here ad these studio, and I show him those dog, and he say he are nize dog, and thad those fire escape he is not *inside*. So I nod break those rule, and he go downstairs spik ad those lady mek those complain, and he say he doan keer if she dam clear out this house. He doan lig' her which even."

Jerry threw up his hands.

"You win, Sunny! Do as you like. Fill the place full if you want to. There's horses and cows to be had if they strike your fancy, and the zoo is full of other kind of live stock. Take your choice."

Sunny, indeed, did proceed to take her choice. It is true she did not bring horses and cows and wild animals into Jerry's apartment; but she passed the word to her doting friends, and in due time the inmates of that duplex apartment made quite a considerable family, with promise of early increase. There was besides Itchy, Count and Countess Taguchi, overfed canaries, who taught Sunny a new kind of whistle; Mr. and Mrs. Satsuma, goldfish who occupied an ornate glass and silver dish, fern and rock lined donated by Jinx, and Miss Spring Morning, a large Persian cat, whom Sunny named after her old friend of the teahouse of a Thousand Joys, but whose name should have been Mr. Spring Morning.

It was a very happy family indeed, and in time the master of the house became quite accustomed to the pets (pests he called them at first), and had that proud feeling moreover of the contented man of family. He often fed the Satsumas and Taguchis himself, and actually was observed to scratch the head of Itchy, who in these days penetrated into the various rooms of the apartment (Sunny having had especial permission from the janitor gentleman) so long as his presence was noiseless. He wore on his scrawny neck a fine leather and gilt collar that Monty sent all the way to Philadelphia to get for Sunny, thereby earning the bitter resentment of his kid brother, who considered that collar his by rightful inheritance from Monty's own recent kid days. Monty's remorse upon "swiping" said collar was shortlived, however, for Sunny's smile and excitement and the fun they had putting it on Itchy more than compensated for any bitter threats of an unreasonable kid brother. Besides Monty brought peace in that disturbed direction by sending the younger Potter a brand new collar, not, it is true, of the history of the one taken, but much more shiny and semi-adjustable.

CHAPTER X

On the 20th of April, Sunny's friend, "Mr. dear Monty" as she called him (J. Lamont Potter, Jr., was his real name), obtained an indefinite leave of absence from the hospital, and called upon Sunny in the absence of Jerry Hammond. He came directly to the object of his call almost as soon as Sunny admitted him. While indeed she was assisting him to remove that nice, loosely hanging taupe coloured spring coat, that looked so well on Monty, he swung around, as his arms came out of his coat sleeves, and made Sunny an offer of his heart and soul. These the girl very regretfully refused. Follows the gist of Sunny's remarks in rejection of the offer:

"Monty, I do not wan' gettin' marry wiz you jos yet, bi-cause you are got two more year to worg on those hospital; then you are got go unto those John Hoppakins for post—something kind worg also. Then you are go ad those college and hospital in Hy——" She tried to say Heidelberg, but the word was too much for her, and he broke in impetuously:

"Listen, Sunny, those *were* my plans, but everything's changed now, since I met you. I've decided to cut it all out and settle down and marry. I've got my degree, and can hang out my shingle. We'll have to economize a bit at first, because the governor, no doubt, will cut me out for doing this; but I'm not in swaddling clothes, and I'll do as I like. So what do you say, Sunny?"

"I say, thas nod ride do those. Your honourable father, he are spend plenty moany for you, and thas unfilial do lig' thad. I thang you, Monty, but I are sawry I kinnod do lig' you ask."

"But look here, Sunny, there are whole heaps of fellows—dubs who never go beyond taking their degree, who go to practising right away, and I can do as they do, as far as that goes, and with you I should worry whether I go up in medicine or not."

"But, Monty, I *wan* see you go up—Ho! up, way high to those top. Thas mos' bes' thing do for gentleman. I do nod lig' man who stay down low on ground. Thas nod nize. I do nod wan' make marry wiz gentleman lig' those."

"We-el, I suppose I could go on with the work and study. If I did, would you wait for me? Would you, Sunny?"

"I do not know, Monty. How I kin see all those year come?"

"Well, but you can promise me, can't you?"

"No, Monty, bi-cause mebbe I goin' die, and then thas break promise. Thas not perlite do lig' those."

"Pshaw! There's no likelihood at all of your dying. You're awfully healthy. Anyone can see it by your colouring. By jove, Sunny, you have the prettiest complexion of any girl I've ever seen. Your cheeks are just like flowers. Die! You're bugs to think of it even. So you are perfectly safe in promising."

"We-el, then I promise that mebbe after those five, six year when you are all troo, *if* I are not marry wiz someone else, then I go *consider* marry wiz you, Monty."

This gracious speech was sweetened by an engaging smile, and Monty, believing that "half a loaf is better than no loaf" showed his pleasure, though his curiosity prompted him to make anxious inquiry as to possible rivals.

"Bobs asked you yet?"

"No—not yet."

"You wouldn't take him if he did, would you, Sunny?"

"No. Not yet."

"Or any time. Say that."

Sunny laughed.

"Any time, Monty."

"And Jinx? What about Jinx?"

"He are always my good friend."

"You wouldn't marry him, would you?"

"No. I are lig' him as frien'."

Monty pursued no further. He knew of the existence of Jerry's Miss Falconer. Dashed, but not hopeless Monty withdrew.

That was on the 20th of April. Bob's proposal followed on the 22nd. He inveigled Sunny into accompanying him to his polished and glorified flat, which was presided over by an ample bosomed and smiling "mammy" whom Bobs had especially imported from the sunny South.

His guest, having exclaimed and enthused over the really cosy and bright little flat, Bobs, with his fine, clever face aglow, asked her to share it with him. The request frightened Sunny. She had exhausted considerable of her stock of excuses against matrimony to Monty, and she did not want to see that look of hope fade from Mr. dear Bobs' face.

"Oh, Bobs, I are *thad* sorry, but me? I do not wan make marry jos yet. Please you waid for some udder day when mebbe perhaps I go change those mind."

"It's all right, Sunny."

Bobs took his medicine like a man, his clean cut face slightly paling, as he followed with a question the lightness of which did not deceive the distressed Sunny:

"You're not engaged to anyone else, are you, Sunny?"

"Emgaged? What are those, Bobs?"

"You haven't promised any other lucky dog that you'll marry him, have you?"

"No-o." Sunny shook her bright head. "No one are ask me yet, 'cept Monty, and I are say same ting to him."

"Good!" Bobs beamed through his disappointment on her.

"While there's life there's hope, you know."

He felt that Jinx's chances were slim, and he, too, knew of Miss Falconer and Jerry.

Sunny, by no means elated by her two proposals, confided in Hatton, and received sage advice:

"Miss Sunny, Hi'm not hin a position exactly to advise you, and hits 'ardly my place, miss, but so long as you hasks my hadvice, I gives it you grattus. Now Mr. Potter, 'ees a trifle young for matrimunny, miss—a trifle young, and Mr. Mapson, I 'ear that 'ees not got hany too much money, and hits a beggarly profession 'ees followin', miss. I 'ave 'eard this from Mr. Jerry's hown folks, 'oo more than once 'as cast haspirations against Mr. Jerry's friends, but hi takes it that wot they're sayin' comes near to the truth habout the newspaper as a perfession, miss. Now there's Mr. Crawford, Miss——"

Hatton's voice took on both a respectful and a confidential tone as he came to Jinx.

"Now, Hi flatters myself that Hi'm some judge of yuman nature, miss, and I make bold to say, hif I may, miss, that Mr. Crawford his about halso to pop the 'appy question to you, miss. Now, hif hi was hin your place, miss, 'ees the gentleman hi'd be after 'ooking. His people hare of the harristocrissy of Hamerica—so far, miss, as Hamerica can 'ave harristocrissy—and Mr. Crawford his the hair to a varst fortune, miss. There's no telling to wot 'eights you might climb if you buckles up with Mr. Crawford, Miss."

"Ho! Hatton, I lig' all those my frien' jos same. Me? I would lig' marry all those, but I kinnod do."

"'Ardly, miss, 'ardly. Hamerica is 'ardly a pollagamous country, though 'hit his the 'ome of the Mormon people."

"Mormon?"

"A church, miss; a sex of people wots given to pollagummy, which is, I takes it, too 'ard and big a word for you, miss, bein' a forriner, to hunderstand, so hi'll explain a bit clearer, miss. The Mormon people hacquire several wives, some helders 'avin' the reputation of bein' in the class with hour hown King 'Enry the Heighth, and worse, miss,—with Solomon 'imself, I 'ave 'eard it said."

"Ho-h-a-!" said Sunny thoughtfully. "Thad is very nize—those Mormon. Thas lig' Japanese emperor. Some time he got lots wife."

Hatton wiped the sweat from his brow. He had gotten upon a subject somewhat beyond his depths, and the young person before him rather scandalised his ideas of what a young lady's views on such matters should be. He had hoped to shock Sunny somewhat. Instead she sighed with an undeniably envious accent as he told her of the reprehensible Mormons. After a moment she asked very softly:

"Hatton, mebbe Jerry ask me those same question."

Hatton turned his back, and fussed with the dishes in the sink. He too knew about Miss Falconer.

"'Ardly, miss, 'ardly."

"Why not, Hatton?"

"If you'll pardon me, I 'ave a great deal of work before me. Hi'm in a 'urry. 'Ave you fed the Count and Countess Taguchi, may I ask, miss."

"Hatton, *if* a man *not* ask girl to make marry wiz him, what she can do?"

"Well now, miss, you got me there. Has far as Hi'm hable to see personally, miss, there haren't nothing left for 'er to do except wait for the leap year."

"Leap year? What are those, Hatton?"

"A hodd year, miss—comes just in so often, miss, due to come next year, halso. When the leap year comes, miss, then the ladies do the popping—they harsks the 'appy question, miss."

"O-h-h-! Thas very nize. I wish it are leap year now," said Sunny wistfully.

"Hit'll come, miss. Hit's on hit's way. A few months and then the ladies' day will dawn," and Hatton, moving about with cheer, clucked at the thought.

CHAPTER XI

A week after Bobs proposed to Sunny, Jinx, shining like the rising sun by an especially careful grooming administered by his valet, a flower adorning his lapel, and a silk hat topping his head, with a box of chocolates large enough to hold an Easter bonnet in his hand, and a smaller box of another kind in his vest pocket, presented himself at Jerry Hammond's studio. Flowers preceded and followed this last of Sunny's ardent suitors.

He was received by a young person arrayed in a pink pongee smock, sleeves rolled up, revealing a pair of dimpled arms, hair in distracting disorder, and a little nose on which seductively perched a blotch of flour, which the infatuated Jinx was requested to waft away with his silken handkerchief.

Sunny's cheeks were flushed from close proximity to that gas stove, and her eyes were bright with the warfare which she waged incessantly upon the aforesaid honourable stove. In the early days of her appearance at the studio—by the way, she had been domiciled there a whole month—Sunny's operations at the gas stove had had disastrous results. Her attempt to boil water by the simple device of turning on the gas, as she did the electric light was alarming in its odorous effects, but her efforts to blow out the oven was almost calamitous, and caused no end of excitement, for it singed her hair and eyebrows and scorched an arm that required the persistent and solicitous attention of her four friends, a doctor and the thoroughly agitated Hatton, on whose head poured the full vials of Jerry's wrath and blame. In fact, this accident almost drove Hatton to desert what he explained to Sunny was the "water wagon."

After that Sunny was strictly ordered by Jerry to keep out of the kitchen. Realising, however, that she could not be trusted on that score, he took half a day off from the office, and gave her a full course of instruction in the mysteries and works of said gas stove. It should be assumed therefore that by this time Sunny should have acquired at least a primary knowledge of the stove. Not so, however. She never lit the oven but she threw salt about to propitiate the oni (goblin) which she was sure had its home somewhere in that strange fire, and she hesitated to touch any of the levers once the fire was lit.

Most of the dishes created by Sunny were more or less under the eye of Hatton, but on this day Hatton had stepped out to the butcher's. Therefore Jinx's arrival was hailed by Sunny with appreciation and relief, and she promptly lead the happy fellow to the kitchen and solicited his advice. Now Jinx, the son of the plutocratic rich, had never been inside a kitchen since his small boyhood, and then his recollection of said portion of the house was of a vast white place, where tiles and marble and white capped cooks prevailed, and small boys were chuckled over or stared at and whispered about.

The dimensions of Sunny's kitchen were about seven by nine feet, and it is well to mention at this moment that the room registered 95 degrees Fahrenheit. Jinx weighed two hundred and forty-five pounds, stripped. His emotions, his preparations, his hurry to enter the presence of his charmer, to say nothing of a volcanic heart, all contributed to add to the heat and discomfort of the fat young man down whose ruddy cheeks the perspiration rolled. Jinx had come upon a mission that in all times in the history of the world, subsequent to cave days, has called for coolness, tact, and as attractive a physical seeming as it is possible to attain.

Sunny drew her friend along to that gas stove, kneeled on the floor, making room for him to kneel beside her—no easy "stunt" for a fat man—opened the lower door and revealed to him the jets on full blaze. Jinx shook his head. The problem was beyond him, but even as his head shook he sniffed a certain fragrant odour that stole directly to a certain point in Jinx's anatomy that Sunny would quaintly have designated as his "honourable insides." The little kitchen, despite its heat, contained in that oven, Jinx knew, that which was more attractive than anything the cool studio could offer. Seating himself heavily on a frail kitchen chair, which creaked ominously under his weight, Jinx awaited hopefully what he felt sure was soon to follow.

In due time Sunny opened the upper door of the oven, withdrew two luscious looking pans of the crispest brown rice cakes, plentifully besprinkled with dates and nuts and over which she dusted powdered sugar, and passing by the really suffering Jinx she transferred the pans to the window ledge, saying with a smile:

"When he are cool, I giving you one, Jinx."

Wiping her hands on the roller towel, she had Jinx pull the smock over her head, and revealed her small person in blue taffeta frock, which Jinx himself had had the honour of choosing for her. Unwillingly, and with one longing backward look at those cakes, Jinx followed Sunny into the studio. Here, removed from the intoxicating effects of that kitchen, Sunny having his full attention again, he came to the object of his call. Jinx sat forward on the edge of his chair, and his round, fat face looked so comically like the man in the moon's that Sunny could not forbear smiling at him affectionately.

"Ho! Jinx, how you are going to lig' those cake when he is getting cold."

Jinx liked them hot just as well. However, he was not such a gourmand that mere rice and date cakes could divert him from the purpose of his call. He sighed so deeply and his expression revealed such a condition of melancholy appeal that Sunny, alarmed, moved over and took his face up in her hand, examining it like a little doctor, head cocked on one side.

"Jinx, you are sick? What you are eat? Show me those tongue!"

"Aw, it's nothing, Sunny—nothing to do with my tongue. It's—it's—just a little heart trouble, Sunny."

"Heart! That are bad place be sick! You are ache on him, Mr. dear Jinx?"

"Ye-eh—some."

"I sawry! How I are sawry! You have see doctor."

"You're the only doctor I need."

Which was true enough. It was surprising the healing effects upon Jinx's aching heart of the solicitous and sympathetic hovering about him of Sunny.

"Oh, Jinx, I go at those telephone ride away, get him Mr. Doctor here come. I 'fraid mebbe you more sick than mebbe you know."

"No, no—never mind a doctor." Jinx held her back by force. "Look-a-here, Sunny, I'll tell you just what's the matter with my heart. I'm—I'm—in love!"

"Oh—love. I have hear those word bi-fore, but I have never feel him," said Sunny wistfully.

"You'll feel it some day all right," groaned Jinx. "And you'll know it too when you've got it."

"Ad Japan nobody—love. Thas not nize word speag ad Japan."

"Gosh! it's the nicest word in the language in America. You can't help speaking it. You can't help feeling it. When you're in love, Sunny, you think day and night and every hour and minute and second of the day of the same person. That's love, Sunny."

"Ah!" whispered Sunny, her eyes very bright and dewey, "I are *know* him then!" And she stood with that rapt look, scarcely hearing Jinx, and brought back to earth only when he took her hand, and clung to it with both his own somewhat flabby ones.

"Sunny, I'm head over heels in love with you. Put me out of my misery. Say you'll be Mrs. Crawford, and you'll see how quickly this old bunged up heart of mine will heal."

"Oh, Jinx, you are ask *me* to make marry wiz you?"

"You bet your life I am. Gosh! I've got an awful case on you, Sunny."

"Ho! I sawry I kinnod do thad to-day. I am not good ad my healt'. Axscuse me. Mebbe some odder day I do so."

"Any day will do. Any day that suits you, if you'll just give me your promise—if you'll just be engaged to me."

"Engaged?" Bobs had already explained to her what that meant, but she repeated it to gain time.

"Why, yes—don't they have engagements in Japan?"

"No. Marriage broker go ad girl's father and boy's father and make those marriage."

"Well, this is a civilised land. We do things right here. You're a lucky girl to have escaped from Japan. Here, in this land, we first get engaged, say for a week or month or even a year—only a short time will do for you and me, Sunny—and then, well, we marry. How about it?"

Sunny considered the question from several serious angles, very thoughtful, very much impressed.

"Jinx, I do nod like to make marriage, bi-cause thas tie me up wiz jos one frien' for hosban'."

"But you don't want more than one husband?"

Jinx remembered hearing somewhere that the Japanese were a polygamous nation, but he thought that only applied to the favoured males of the race.

"No—O thas very nize for Mormon man I am hear of, bud———"

"Not fit for a woman," warmly declared Jinx. "All I ask of you, Sunny, is that you'll promise to marry me. If you'll do that, you'll make me the happiest bug in these United States. I'll be all but looney, and that's a fact."

"I sawry, Jinx, but me? I kinnod do so."

Jinx relapsed into a state of the darkest gloom. Looking out from the depths of the big, soft overstuffed chair, he could see not a gleam of light, and presently groaned:

"I suppose if I weren't such a mass of flesh and fat, I might stand a show with you. It's hell to be fat, I'll tell the world."

"Jinx, I lig' those fat. It grow nize on you. And *pleass* do not loog so sad on you face. Wait, I go get you something thas goin' make you look smile again."

She disappeared into the kitchen, returning with the whole platter of cookies, still quite warm, and irresistibly odorous and toothsome looking. Jinx, endeavouring to refuse, had to close his eyes to steady him in his resolve, but he could not close his nose, nor his mouth either, when Sunny thrust one of the delicious pieces into his mouth. She wooed him back to a semi-normal condition by feeding him crisp morsels of his favourite confection, nor was it possible to resist something that pushed against one's mouth, and once having entered that orifice revealed qualities that appealed to the very best in one's nature.

Jinx was not made of the Spartan stuff of heroes, and who shall blame him if nature chose to endow him with a form of rich proportions that included "honourable insides" whose capacity was unlimited. So, till the very last cooky, and a sense of well being and fulness, the sad side of life pushed aside _pro tem_, Jinx was actually able to smile indulgently at the solicitous Sunny. She clapped her hands delightedly over her success. Jinx's fingers found their way to his vest pocket. He withdrew a small velvet box, and snapped back the lid. Silently he held it toward Sunny. Her eyes wide, she stared at it with excited rapture.

"Oh-h! Thas mos' beautifullest thing I are ever see."

Never, in fact, had her eyes beheld anything half so lovely as that shining platinum work of art with its immense diamond.

"Just think," said Jinx huskily, "if you say the word, you can have stones like that covering you all over."

"All over!" She made an expressive motion of her hands which took in all of her small person.

Melancholy again clouded Jinx's face. After all, he did not want Sunny to marry him for jewelry.

"I tell you what you do, Sunny. Wear this for me, will you? Wear it for a while, anyway, and then when you decide finally whether you'll have me or not, keep it or send it back, as you like."

He had slipped the ring onto the third finger of Sunny's left hand, and holding that had made him a bit bolder. Sunny, unsuspecting and sympathetic, let her hand rest in his, the ring up, where she could admire it to her heart's content.

"Look a here, Sunny, will you give me a kiss, then—just one. The ring's worth that, isn't it?"

Sunny retreated hurriedly, almost panically?

"Oh, Jinx, please you excuse me to-day, bi-cause I *lig'* do so, but Mr. Hatton he are stand ad those door and loog on you."

"Damn Hatty!" groaned Jinx bitterly, and with a sigh that heaved his big breast aloft, he picked up his hat and cane, and ponderously moved toward the door.

In the lower hall of the studio apartment, who should the crestfallen Jinx encounter but his old-time friend, Jerry Hammond, returning from his eight hours' work at the office. His friend's greeting was both curt and cold, and there was no mistaking that look of dislike and disapproval that the frowning face made no effort to disguise.

"Here again, Jinx. Better move in," was Jerry's greeting.

Jinx muttered something inarticulate and furious, and for a fat man he made quick time across the hall and out into the street, where he climbed with a heavy heart into the great roadster, which he had fondly hoped might also carry Sunny with him upon a prolonged honeymoon.

CHAPTER XII

Sunny poured Jerry's tea with a hand turned ostentatiously in a direction that revealed to his amazed and indignant eye that enormous stone of fire that blazed on the finger of Sunny's left hand. His appetite, always excellent, failed him entirely, and after conquering the first surge of impulses that were almost murderous, he lapsed into an ominous silence, which no guile nor question from the girl at the head of his table could break. A steady, a cold, a biting glare, a murmured monosyllabic reply was all the response she received to her amiable overtures. His ill temper, moreover, reached out to the inoffensive Hatton, whom he ordered to clear out, and stay out, and if it came down to that get out altogether, rather than hang around snickering in that way. Thus Jerry revealed a side to his character hitherto unsuspected by Sunny, though several rumblings and barks from the "dog in the manger" would have apprized one less innocent than she.

They finished that meal—or rather Sunny did—in silence electric with coming strife. Then Jerry suddenly left the table, strode into the little hall, took down his hat and coat, and was about to go, heaven knows where, when Sunny, at his elbow, sought to restrain him by force. She took his sleeve and tenaciously held to it, saying:

"Jerry, do not go out these night. I are got some news I lig' tell to you."

"Let go my arm. I'm not interested in your news. I've a date of my own."

"But Jerry——"

"I say, let go my arm, will you?"

The last was said in a rising voice, as he reached the crest of irritation, and jerking his sleeve so roughly from her clasp, he accomplished the desired freedom, but the look on Sunny's face stayed with him all the way down those apartment stairs—he ignored the elevator—and to the door of the house. There he stopped short, and without more ado, retraced his steps, sprang up the stairs in a great hurry, and jerking open his door again, Jerry returned to his home. He discovered Sunny curled on the floor, with her head buried in the seat of his favourite chair—the one occupied that afternoon by the mischief-making Jinx.

"Sunny! I'm awfully sorry I was such a beast. Say, little girl, look here, I'm not myself. I don't know what I'm doing."

Sunny slowly lifted her face, revealing to the relieved but indignant Jerry a face on which it is true there were traces of a tear or two, but which nevertheless smiled at him quite shamelessly and even triumphantly. Jerry felt foolish, and he was divided between a notion to remain at home with the culprit—she had done nothing especially wrong, but he felt that she was to blame for something or other—or follow his first intention of going out for the night—just where, he didn't know—but anywhere would do to escape the thought that had come to him—the thought of Sunny's probable engagement to Jinx. However, Sunny gave him no time to debate the matter of his movements for the evening. She very calmly assisted him to remove his coat, hung up his hat, and when she had him comfortably ensconced in his favourite chair, had herself lit his pipe and handed it to him, she drew up a stool and sat down in front of his knees, just as if, in fact, she was entirely guiltless of an engagement of which Jerry positively did not intend to approve. Her audacity, moreover, was such that she did not hesitate to lay her left hand on Jerry's knee, where he might get the full benefit of the radiant light from that ring. He looked at it, set down his pipe on the stand at his elbow, and stirred in that restless way which portends hasty arising, when Sunny:

"Jerry, Jinx are come to-day to ask me make marriage with him."

"The big stiff. I pity any girl that has to go through life with that fathead."

"Ho! I are always lig' thad fat grow on Jinx. It look very good on him. I are told him so."

"Matter of taste of course," snarled Jerry, fascinated by the twinkling of that ring in spite of himself, and feeling at that moment an emotion that was dangerously like hatred for the girl he had done so much for.

"Monty and Bobs are also ask me marry wiz them." Sunny dimpled quite wickedly at this, but Jerry failed to see any humour in the matter. He said with assumed loftiness:

"Well, well, proposals raining down on you in every direction. Your janitor gentleman and landlord asked you too?"

"No-o, not yit, but those landlord are say he lig' take me for ride some nize days on his car ad those park."

"The hell he did!"

Jerry sat up with such a savage jerk at this that he succeeded in upsetting the innocent hand resting so confidingly upon his knee.

"Who asked him around here anyway?" demanded Jerry furiously. "Just because he owns this building doesn't mean he has a right to impose himself on the tenants, and I'll tell him so damn quick."

"But, Jerry, *I* are ask him come up here. Itchy fall down on those fire escape, and he are making so much noise on this house when he cry, that everybody who live on this house open those windows on court, and I are run down quick on those fire escape and everybody also run out see what's all those trouble. Then I am cry so hard, bi-cause I are afraid Itchy are hurt himself too bad, bi-cause he also are cry very loud." Sunny lifted her nose sky-ward, illustrating how the dog's cries had emanated from him. "So then, everybody *very* kind at me and Itchy, and the janitor gentleman carry him bag ad these room, and the landlord gentleman say thas all ride henceforth I have thad little dog live wiz me ad these room also. He say it is very hard for liddle girl come from country way off be 'lone all those day, and mebbe some day he take me and Itchy for ride ad those park. So I are say, 'Thang you, I will like go vaery much, thang you.'"

"Well, make up your mind to it, you're not going, do you understand? I'll have no landlords taking you riding in any parks."

Having delivered this ultimatum as viciously as the circumstances called for, Jerry leaned back in pretended ease and awaited further revelations from Sunny.

"—but," went on Sunny, as if finishing a sentence, "that landlord gentleman are not also ask me marry wiz him, Jerry. He already got big wife. I are see her. She are so big as Jinx, and she smile on me very kind, and say she have hear of me from her hosban', that I am very lonely girl from Japan, and thas very sad for me, and she goin' to take those ride wiz me also."

"Hm!" Jerry felt ashamed of himself, but he did not propose to reveal it, especially when that little hand had crept back to its old place on his knee, and the diamond flaunted brazenly before his gaze. Nobody but a "fat-head" would buy a diamond of that size anyway, was Jerry's opinion. There was something extremely vulgar about diamonds. They were not nearly as pretty as rubies or emeralds or even turquoise, and Jerry had never liked them. Of course, Miss Falconer, like every other girl, had to have her diamond, and Jerry recalled with irritation how, as a sophomore, he had purchased that first diamond. He neither enjoyed the expedition nor the memory of it. Jinx's brazen ring made him think of Miss Falconer's. However, the thought of Miss Falconer was, for some reason or other, distasteful to Jerry in these days, and, moreover, the girl before him called for his full attention as usual.

"So you decided on Jinx, did you? Bobs and Monty in the discard and the affluent fat and fair Jinx the winner."

"Jerry, I are *prefer* marry all my friends, but I say 'no' to each one of those."

"What are you wearing Jinx's ring for then?"

"Bi-cause it are loog nize on my hands, and he *ask* me wear it there."

New emotions were flooding over the contrite Jerry. Something was racing like champagne through his veins, and he suddenly realised how "damnably jolly" life was after all. Still, even though Sunny had admitted that no engagement existed between her and Jinx, there was that ring. Poor little girl! A fellow had to teach her all of the western conventions, she was that innocent and simple.

"Sunny, you don't want to wear a fellow's ring unless you intend to marry him, don't you understand that? The ring means that you are promised to him, do you get me?"

"No! But I *are* promise to Jinx. I are promise that I will consider marry him some day if I do not marry some other man I *wan'* ask me also."

"Another man. Who———?"

Sunny's glance directed full upon him left nothing to the imagination. Jerry's heart began to thump in a manner that alarmed him.

"Jerry," said Sunny, "I going to wear Jinx's ring *until* that man also asking me. I *wan* him do so, bi-cause I are lig' him mos' bes' of all my frien'. I think———" She had both of her hands on his knees now, and was leaning up looking so wistfully into his face that he tried to avert his own gaze. In spite of the lump that rose in his throat, in spite of the frantic beating of his heart, Jerry did not ask the question that the girl was waiting to hear. After a moment, she said gently:

"Jerry, Hatty are tell me that nex' year he are come a Leap. Then, he say, thas perlite for girl ask man make marriage wiz her. Jerry, *I* are goin' to wait till those year of Leap are come, and then, me? I are goin' ask *you* those question."

For one thrilling moment there was a great glow in the heart of Jerry Hammond, and then his face seemed suddenly to turn grey and old. His voice was husky and there was a mist before his eyes.

"Sunny, I must tell you—Sunny, I—I—am already engaged to be married to an American girl—a girl my people want me to marry. I've been engaged to her since my eighteenth year. I—*don't* look at me like that, Sunny, or——"

The girl's head dropped to the level of the floor, her hands slipping helplessly from his knees. She seemed all in a moment to become purely Japanese. There was that in her bowed head that was strangely reminiscent of some old and vanished custom of her race. She did not raise her head, even as she spoke:

"I wishin' you ten thousand year of joy. Sayonara for this night."

Sunny had left him alone. Jerry felt the inability to stir. He stared into the dying embers of his fire with the look of one who has seen a vision that has disappeared ere he could sense its full significance. It seemed at that moment to Jerry as if everything desirable and precious in life were within reach, but he was unable to seize it. It was like his dream of beauty, ever above, but beyond man's power to completely touch. Sunny was like that, as fragile, as elusive as beauty itself. The thought of his having hurt Sunny tore his heart. She had aroused in him every impulse that was chivalrous. The longing to guard and cherish her was paramount to all other feelings. What was it Professor Barrowes had warned him of? That he should refrain from taking the bloom from the rose. Had he, then, all unwittingly, injured little Sunny?

Mechanically, Jerry went into the hall, slowly put his hat on his head and passed out into the street. He walked up and down 67th Street and along Central Park West to 59th Street, retracing his steps three times to the studio building, and turning back again. His mind was in a chaos, and he knew not what to do. Only one clear purpose seemed to push through the fog, the passionate determination to care for Sunny. She came first of all. Indeed she occupied the whole of his thought. The claim of the girl who had waited for him seven years seemed of minor importance when compared with the claim of the girl he loved. The disinclination to hurt another had kept him from breaking an engagement that had never been of his own desire, but now Jerry knew there could be no more evasions. The time had come when he must face the issue squarely. His sense of honour demanded that he make a clean breast of the entire matter to Miss Falconer. He reached this resolve while still walking on 59th Street. It gave him no more than time to catch the night train to Greenwich. As he stepped aboard the train that was bearing him from Sunny to Miss Falconer all of the fogs had cleared from Jerry's mind. He was conscious of an immense sense of relief. It seemed strange to him that he had never taken this step before. Judging the girl by himself, he felt that he knew exactly what she would say when with complete candour he should "lay his cards upon the table." He felt sure that she was a good sport. He did not delude himself with the idea that an engagement that had been irksome to himself had been of any joy to her. It was simply, so he told himself, a mistake of their parents. They had planned and worked this scheme, and into it they had dumped these two young people at a psychological moment.

CHAPTER XIII

For two days Sunny waited for Jerry to return. She was lonely and most unhappy, but hers was a buoyant personality, and withal her hurt she kept up a bright face before her little world of that duplex studio. In spite of the two nights when no sleep at all came, and she lay through the long hours trying vainly not to think of the wife of Jerry Hammond, in the daytime she moved about the small concerns of the apartment with a smile of cheer and found a measure of comfort in her pets.

It was all very well, however, to hug Itchy passionately to her breast, and assure herself that she had in her arms one true and loving friend. Always she set the dog sadly down again, saying:

"Ah, liddle honourable dog, you are jos liddle dog, thas all. How you can know whas ache on my heart. I do nod lig' you more for to-day."

She fed Mr. and Mrs. Satsuma, and whistled and sang to them. After all, a canary is only a canary. Its bright, hard eye is blank and cold. Even the goldfish, swimming to the top of the honourable bowl, and picking the crumb so cunningly from her finger, lost their charm for her. Miss Spring Morning had long since been vanished with severe Japanese reproaches for his inhuman treatment of Sunny's first friends, the honourable mice, several of whose little bodies Sunny had confided to a grave she herself had dug, with tears that aroused the janitor gentleman's sympathy, so that he permitted the interment in the back yard.

The victrola, working incessantly the first day, supplied merely noise. On the second morning she banged the top impulsively down, and cried at Caruso:

"Oh, I do not wan' hear your honourable voice to-day. Shut you up!"

Midway in an aria from "Rigoletto" the golden voice was quenched.

She hovered about the telephone, and several times lifted the receiver, with the idea of calling one of her friends, but always she rejected the impulse. Intuitively Sunny knew that until the first pang of her refusal had passed her friends were better away from her.

Little comfort was to be extracted from Hatton, who was acting in a manner that had Sunny not been so absorbed by her own personal trouble would have caused her concern. Hatton talked incessantly and feverishly and with tears about his Missus, and what she had driven him to, and of how a poor man tries to do his duty in life, but women were ever trouble makers, and it was only "yuman nature" for a man to want a little pleasure, and he, Hatton, had made this perfectly clear to Mr. Hammond when he had taken service with him.

"A yuman being, miss," said Hatton, "is yuman, and that's all there is to it. Yuman nature 'as certain 'ankerings and its against yuman nature to gainsay them 'ankerings, if you'll pardon me saying so, miss."

However, he assured Sunny most earnestly that he was fighting the Devil and all his works, which was just what "them 'ankerings" was, and he audibly muttered for her especial hearing in proof of his assertion several times through the day: "Get thee be'ind me, Satan." Satan being "them 'ankerings, miss."

In normal times Sunny's fun and cheer would have been of invaluable assistance and diversion to Hatton. Indeed, his long abstention was quite remarkable since she had been there; but Sunny, affect cheer as she might, could not hide from the sympathetic Hatton's gaze the fact that she was most unhappy. In fact, Sunny's sadness affected the impressionable Hatton so that the second morning he could stand it no longer, and disappeared for several hours, to return, hiccoughing cravenly, and explaining:

"I couldn't 'elp it, miss. My 'eart haches for you, and it ain't yuman nature to gainsay the yuman 'eart."

"Hatton," said Sunny severely, "I are smell you on my nose. You are not smell good."

"Pardon me, miss," said Hatton, beginning to weep. "Hi'm sadly ashamed of myself, miss. If you'll pardon me, miss, I'll betake myself to less 'appy regions than Mr. 'Ammond's studio, miss, 'as it's my desire not to 'urt your sense of smell, miss. So if you'll pardon me, I'll say good-bye, miss, 'oping you'll be in a 'appier mood when next we meet."

For the rest of that day there was no further sign from Hatton. Left thus alone in the apartment, Sunny was sore put to find something to distract her, for all the old diversions, without Jerry, began to pall. She wished wistfully that Jerry had not forbidden her to make friends with other tenants in the house. She felt the strange need of a friend at this hour. There was one woman especially whom Sunny would have liked to know better. She always waved to Sunny in such a friendly way across the court, and once she called across to her: "Do come over and see me. I want you to see some of the sketches I have made of you at the window." Sunny pointed the lady out to Jerry, and that young man's face became surprisingly inflamed and he ordered Sunny so angrily not to continue an acquaintance with her unknown friend, that the poor child avoided going near the window for fear of giving offence.

Also, there was a gentleman who came and went periodically in the studio building, and whose admiring looks had all but embraced Sunny even before she scraped an acquaintance with him. He did not live in this building, but came very frequently to call upon certain of the artists, including the lady across the court. Like Jinx, he always wore a flower in his buttonhole, but, unlike Jinx, his clothes had a certain distinction that to the unsophisticated Sunny seemed to spell the last word in style. She was especially fascinated by his tan-coloured spats, and once, examining them with earnest curiosity while waiting for the elevator, her glance arose to his face, and she met his all embracing smile with one of her own engaging ones. This man was in fact a well known dilettante and man about town, a dabbler a bit himself in the arts, but a monument of egotism. He had diligently built up a reputation as a patron and connoisseur of art.

One Sunday morning Sunny came in from a little walk as far as the park, with Itchy. In spite of an unexpectedly hard shower that had fallen soon after she had left, she returned smiling and perfectly dry; excited and delighted moreover over the fortune that had befallen her.

"Jerry!" she cried as soon as she entered, "I are git jost to those corner, when down him come those rain. So much blow! Futen (the wind god) get very angery and blow me quick up street, but the rain fall down jos' lig' cloud are burst. Streets flow lig' grade river. Me? I are run quick and come up on steps of house, and there are five, ten other people also stand on those step and keep him dry. One gentleman he got beeg umberella. I feel sure that umberella it keep me dry. So I smile on those mans———"

"You *what?*"

"I make a smile on him. Like these———" Sunny illustrated innocently.

"Don't you know better than to smile at any man on the street?"

Sunny was taken aback. The Japanese are a smiling nation, and the interchange of smiles among the sexes is not considered reprehensible; certainly not in the class from which Sunny had come.

"Smile are not bad. He are kind thing, Jerry. It make people feel happy, and it do lots good on those worl'. When I smile on thad gentlemen, he are smile ride bag on me ad once, and he take me by those arm, and say he bring me home all nize and dry. And, Jerry, he say, he thing I am too nize piece—er—brick-brack—" bric-a-brac was a new word for Sunny, but Jerry recognised what she was trying to say—"to git wet. So he give me all those umberella. He bring me ride up ad these door, and he say he come see me very soon now as he lig' make sure I got good healt'. He are a very kind gentleman, Jerry. Here are his card."

Jerry took the card, glared at it, and began panically walking up and down the apartment, raging and roaring like an "angery tiger," as Sunny eloquently described him to herself, and then flung around on her and read her such a scorching lecture that the girl turned pale with fright, and, as usual, the man was obliged to swallow his steam before it was all exploded.

In parenthesis, it may be here added, that the orders given by Jerry to that black boy at the telephone desk, embraced such a diabolical description of the injury that was destined to befall him should the personage in question ever step his foot across Jerry's threshold, that Sambo, his eyes rolling, never failed to assure the caller, who came very persistently thereafter, that "Dat young lady she am move away, sah. Yes, sah, she am left this department."

It will be seen, therefore, that Sunny, a stranger in a strange land, shut in alone in a studio, religiously following the instructions of Jerry to refrain from making acquaintances with anyone about her, was in a truly sad state. She started to houseclean, but stopped midway in panic, recalling the Japanese superstition that to clean or sweep a house when one of the family is absent is to precipitate bad fortune upon the house. So she got down all of Jerry's clothes and piously pressed and sponged them, as she had seen Hatton do, being very careful this time to avoid her first mistake in ironing. So earnestly had she applied herself to ironing the crease in the front of one of Jerry's trousers that first time that a most disastrous accident was the result. Jerry, wearing the pressed trousers especially to please her, found himself on the street the cynosure of all eyes as he manfully strode along with a complete split down the front of one of the legs, which the too ardent iron of Sunny had scorched. Having brushed and cleaned all of Jerry's clothes on this day, she prepared her solitary lunch; but this she could not eat. Thoughts of Jerry sharing with her the accustomed meals was too much for the imaginative Sunny, and pushing the rice away from her, she said:

"Oh, I do nod lig' put food any more ad my insides. I givin you to my friends."

The contents of her bowl were emptied into the pail under the sink, which she kept always so clean, for she still was under the delusion that said pail helped to feed the janitor gentleman and his family.

All of that afternoon hung heavily on her hands, and she vainly sought something to interest her and divert her mind from the thought of Jerry. She found herself unconsciously listening for the bell, but, curiously enough, all of that day neither the buzzer, the telephone nor even the dumbwaiter rang. She made a tour of exploration to Jerry's sacred room, lovingly arranging his pieces on his chiffonier, and washing her hands in some toilet water that especially appealed to her. Then she found the bottle of hair tonic. Sniffing it, she decided it was very good, and, painfully, Sunny deciphered the legend printed on the outside, assuring a confiding hair world that the miraculous contents had the power to remove dandruff, invigorate, strengthen, force growth on bald heads, cause to curl and in every way improve and cause to shine the hair of the fortunate user of the same.

"Thas very good stuff," said Sunny. "He do grade miracle on top those head."

She decided to put the shampoo-tonic to the test, and accordingly washed her hair in Jerry's basin, making an excellent job of it. Descending to the studio, she lit the fireplace, and curled up on a big Navaho by the fire. Wrapped in a gorgeous bathrobe belonging to Jerry, Sunny proceeded to dry her hair.

While she was in the midst of this process, the telephone rang. Sambo at the desk announced that visitors were ascending. Sunny had no time to dress or even to put up her hair, and when in response to the sharp bang upon the knocker she opened the door she revealed to the callers a vision that justified their worst fears. Her hair unbound, shining and springing out in lovely curling disorder about her, wrapped about in the bright embroidered bathrobe which the younger woman recognised at once as her Christmas gift to her fiancé, the work, in fact, of her own hands, Sunny was a spectacle to rob a rival of complete hope and peace of mind. The cool fury of unrequited love and jealousy in the breast of the younger woman and the indignant anger in that of the older was whipped at the sight of Sunny into active and violent eruption.

"What are you doing in my son's apartment?" demanded the mother of Jerry, raising to her eyes what looked to Sunny like a gold stick on which grew a pair of glasses, and surveying with pronounced disapproval the politely bowing though somewhat flurried Sunny.

"I are live ad those house," said Sunny, simply. "This are my home."

"You live here, do you? Well, I would have you know that I am the mother of the young man whose life you are ruining, and this young girl is his fiancée."

"Ho! I am very glad make you 'quaintance," said Sunny, seeking to hide behind a politeness her shock at the discovery of the palpable rudeness of these most barbarian ladies. It was hard for her to admit that the ladies of Jerry's household were not models of fine manners, as she had fondly supposed, but on the contrary bore faces that showed no trace of the kind hearts which the girl from Japan had been taught by her mother to associate always with true gentility. The two women's eyes met with that exclamatory expression which says plainer than words:

"Of all the unbounded impudence, this is the worst!"

"I have been told," went on Mrs. Hammond haughtily, "that you are a foreigner—a Japanese." She pronounced the word as if speaking of something extremely repellent.

Sunny bowed, with an attempted smile, that faded away as Jerry's mother continued ruthlessly:

"You do not look like a Japanese to me, unless you have been peroxiding your hair. In my opinion you are just an ordinary everyday bad girl."

Sunny said very faintly:

"Aexcuse me!"

She turned like a hurt thing unjustly punished to the other woman, as if seeking help there. It had been arranged between the two women that Mrs. Hammond was to do the talking. Miss Falconer was having her full of that curious satisfaction some women take in seeing in person one's rival. Her expression far more moved Sunny than that of the angry older woman.

"No one but a bad woman," went on Mrs. Hammond, "would live like this in a young man's apartment, or allow him to support her, or take money from him. Decent girls don't do that sort of thing in America. You are old enough to get out and earn for yourself an honest living. Aren't you ashamed of yourself? Or are you devoid of shame, you bad creature?"

"Yes," said Sunny, with such a look that Jerry's mother's frown relaxed somewhat: "I are ashame. I are sawry thad I are bad—woman. Aexcuse me this time. I try do better. I sawry I are—bad!"

This was plainly a full and complete confession of wrong and its effect on the older woman was to arouse a measure of the Hammond compunction which always followed a hasty judgment. For a moment Mrs. Hammond considered the advisability of reading to this girl a lecture that she had recently prepared to deliver before an institution for the welfare of such girls as she deemed Sunny to be. However, her benevolent intention was frustrated by Miss Falconer.

There is a Japanese proverb which says that the tongue three inches long can kill a man six feet tall, but the tongue of one's enemy is not the worst thing to fear. The cold smile of the young woman staring so steadily at her had power to wound Sunny far more than the lacerating tongue of the woman whom she realised believed she was fighting in her son's behalf. Very silken and soft was the manner of Miss Falconer as insinuatingly she brought Mrs. Hammond back to the object of their call. She had used considerable tact and strategy in arranging this call upon Sunny, having in fact induced Jerry to remain for at least a day or two in Greenwich, "to think matters over," and see "whether absence would not prove to him that what he imagined to be love was nothing but one of those common aberrations to which men who lived in the east were said to be addicted." Jerry, feeling that he should at least do this for her, waited at Greenwich. Miss Falconer had called in the able and belligerent aid of his mother.

"Mother, dear——" She already called Mrs. Hammond "mother." "Suppose—er—we make a quick end to the matter. You know what we are here for. Do let us finish and get away. You know, dear, that I am not used to this sort of thing, and really I'm beginning to get a nervous headache."

Stiffened and upheld by the young woman whom she had chosen as wife for her son, Mrs. Hammond delivered the ultimatum.

"Young woman, I want you to pack your things and clear out from my son's apartment at once. No argument! No excuses! If you do not realise the shamelessness of the life you are leading, I have nothing further to say; but I insist, insist most emphatically, on your leaving my boy's apartment this instant."

A key turned in the lock. Hatton, dusty and bedraggled, his hat on one side of his head and a cigarette twisting dejectedly in the corner of his mouth, stumbled in at the door. He stood swaying and smiling at the ladies, stuttering incoherent words of greeting and apology.

"La-adiesh, beggin' y'r pardon, it's a pleasure shee thish bright shpring day."

Mrs. Hammond, overwhelmed with shame and grief over the revelation of the disreputable inmates of her son's apartment, turned her broad back upon Hatton. She recognised that man. He was the man she and Jerry's father had on more than one occasion begged their son to be rid of. Oh! if only Jeremy Hammond senior were here now!

Sunny, having heard the verdict of banishment, stood helplessly, like one who has received a death sentence, knowing not which way to turn. Hatton staggered up the stairs, felt an uncertain course along the gallery toward his room, and fell in a muddled heap midway of the gallery.

Sunny, half blindly, scarcely conscious of what she was doing, had moved with mechanical obedience toward the door, when Mrs. Hammond haughtily recalled her.

"You cannot go out on the street in that outrageous fashion. Get your things, and do your hair up decently. We will wait here till you are ready."

"And suppose you take that bathrobe off. It doesn't belong to you," said Miss Falconer cuttingly.

"Take only what belongs to you," said Mrs. Hammond.

Sunny slowly climbed up to her room. Everything appeared now strange and like a queer dream to her. She could scarcely believe that she was the same girl who but a few days before had joyously flitted about the pretty room, which showed evidence of her intensely artistic and feminine hands. She changed from the bathrobe to the blue suit she had worn on the night she had arrived at Jerry's studio. From a drawer she drew forth the small package containing the last treasures that her mother had placed in her hand. Though she knew that Mrs. Hammond and Miss Falconer were impatiently awaiting her departure, she sat down at her desk and painfully wrote her first letter to Jerry.

"Jerry sama: How I thank you three and four time for your kindness to me. I am sorry I are not got money to pay you back for all that same, but I will take nothing with me but those clothes on my body. Only bad girls take money from gentleman at this America. I have hear that to-day, but I never know that before, or I would not do so. I have pray to Amaterasu-oho-mikami, making happy sunshine of your life. May you live ten thousand year. Sayonara. Sunny."

She came out along the gallery, bearing her mother's little package. Kneeling by the half-awake but helpless Hatton she thrust the letter into his hand.

"Good-bye, kind Hatton," said Sunny. "I sawry I not see your face no more. I sawry I are make all those trobble for you wiz those gas stove an' those honourable mice. I never do those ting again. I hope mebbe you missus come home agin some day ad you. Sayonara."

"Wh-wheer y're goin', Shunny. Whatsh matter?" Hatton tried vainly to raise himself. He managed to pull himself a few paces along, by holding to the gallery rails, but sprawled heavily down on the floor. The indignant voice of his master's mother ascended from the stairs:

"If you do not control yourself, my good man, I will be forced to call in outside aid and have you incarcerated."

Downstairs, Sunny, unmindful of the waiting women, ran by them into the kitchen. From goldfish to canaries she turned, whispering softly: "Sayonara my friends. I sawry leaving you."

She was opening the window onto the fire-escape, and Itchy with a howl of joy had leaped into her arms, when Mrs. Hammond and Miss Falconer, suspicious of something underhand, appeared at the door.

"What are you doing, miss? What is that you are taking?" demanded Mrs. Hammond.

Sunny turned, with her dog hugged up close to her breast.

"I are say good-bye to my liddle dog," she said. "Sayonara Itchy. The gods be good unto you."

She set the dog hastily back in the box, against his most violent protests, and Itchy immediately set up such a woeful howling and baying as only a small mongrel dog who possesses psychic qualities and senses the departure of an adored one could be capable of. Windows were thrown up and ejaculations and protests emanated from tenants in the court, but Sunny had clapped both hands over her ears, and without a look back at her little friend, and ignoring the two women, she ran through the studio, and out of the front door.

After her departure a silence fell between Miss Falconer and Mrs. Hammond. The latter's face suddenly worked spasmodically, and the strain of the day overtook Jerry's mother. She sobbed unrestrainedly, mopping up the tears that coursed down her face. Miss Falconer fanned herself slowly, and with an absence of her usual solicitude for her prospective mother-in-law, she refrained from offering sympathy to the older woman, who presently said in a muffled voice:

"Oh, Stella, I am afraid that we may have done a wrong act. It's possible that we have made a mistake about this girl. She seemed so very young, and her face—it was not a bad face, Stella—quite the contrary, now I think of it."

"Well, I suppose that's the way you look at it. Personally you can't expect me to feel any sort of sympathy for a bad woman like that."

"Stella, I've been thinking that a girl who would say good-bye to her dog like that cannot be wholly bad."

"I have heard of murderers who trained fleas," said Miss Falconer. Then, with a pretended yawn, she added, "But really we must be going now? It's getting very dark out, and I'm dining with the Westmores at seven. I told Matthews we'd be through shortly. He's at the curb now."

She had picked up her gloves and was drawing them smoothly on, when Mrs. Hammond noticed the left hand was ringless.

"Why, my dear, where is your ring?"

"Why, you didn't suppose, did you, that I was going to continue my engagement to Jerry Hammond after what he told me?"

"But our purpose in coming here———"

"*My* purpose was to make sure that if *I* were not to have Jerry neither should she—that Japanese doll!" All the bottled-up venom of the girl's nature came forth in that single utterance. "Do let us get away. Really I'm bored to extinction."

"You may go any time you choose, Miss Falconer," said Jerry Hammond's mother. "I shall stay here till my son returns."

It was less than half an hour later that Jerry burst into the studio. He came in with a rush, hurrying across the big room toward the kitchen and calling aloud:

"Sunny! Hi! Sunny! I'm back!"

So intent was he in discovering Sunny that he did not see his mother, sitting in the darkened room by the window. Through dim eyes Mrs. Hammond had been staring into the street, and listening to the nearby rumble of the Sixth Avenue elevated trains. Somehow the roar of the elevated spelled to the woman the cruelty and the power of the mighty city, out into which she had driven the young girl, whose eyes had entreated her like a little wounded creature. The club woman thought of her admonitions and speeches to the girls she had professionally befriended, yet here, put to a personal test, she had failed signally.

Her son was coming through the studio again, calling up toward the gallery above:

"Hi! Sunny, old scout, where are you?"

He turned, with a start, as his mother called his name. His first impulse of welcome halted as he saw her face, and electrically there flashed through Jerry a realisation of the truth. His mother's presence there was connected with Sunny's absence.

"Mother, where is Sunny? What are you doing here? Where is Sunny, I say?"

He shot the questions at her frantically. Mrs. Hammond began to whimper, dabbing at her face with her handkerchief.

"For heaven's sake, answer me. What have you done with Sunny?"

"Jerry, how can I tell you? Jerry—Miss Falcon-er and I—we—we thought it was for your good. I didn't realise that you c-cared so much about her, and I—and we——Oh-h-h," she broke down, crying uncontrolledly, "we have driven that poor little girl out—into the street."

"You what? What is that you say?"

He stared at his mother with a look of loathing.

"Jerry, I thought—we thought her bad and we——"

"Bad! *Sunny!* Bad! She didn't know what the word meant. My *God!*"

He leaped up the stairs, calling the girl's name aloud, as if to satisfy himself that his mother's story was false, but her empty room told its own tale, and half way across the gallery he came upon Hatton. He kicked the valet awake, and the latter raised up, stuttering and blubbering, and extending with shaking hand the letter Sunny had left. The words leaped up at him and smote him to the soul. He did not see his mother. He did not hear her cries, imploring him not to go out like that. Blindly, his heart on fire, Jerry Hammond dashed out from his studio, and plunged into the darkening street, to begin his search for the lost Sunny, who had disappeared into that maelstrom that is New York.

CHAPTER XIV

Despite all that money and influence could do to aid in the search of the missing girl, no trace of Sunny had been found since the day she passed through the door of the studio apartment and disappeared into the seething throngs under the Sixth Avenue elevated.

Every policeman in Manhattan, Brooklyn and the Bronx; every private detective in the country, and the police and authorities throughout the country, aided in that search, keen to earn the enormous rewards offered by her friends. Jerry's entire fortune was at the disposal of the department. Jinx had instructed them to "go the limit" as far as he was concerned. Bobs, his newspaper instinct keyed up to the highest tension, saw in every clue a promise of a solution, and "covered" the disappearance day and night. Young Monty, changed from the cheeriest interne at Bellevue to the most pessimistic and gloomy, developed a weird passion for the morgue, and spent hours hovering about that ghastly part of the hospital.

The four young men met each night at Jerry's studio and cast up their barren results. Jinx unashamedly and even noisily wept, the big tears splashing down his no longer ruddy cheeks. Jinx had honestly loved Sunny, and her loss was the first serious grief of his life.

Monty hugged his head and ruminated over the darkest possibilities. He had suggested to the police that they drag certain parts of the Hudson River, and was indignant when they pointed out the impracticability of such a thing. In the spring the great river was swollen to its highest, and flowing along at a great speed, it would have been impossible to find what Monty suggested.

Jerry, of all her friends, had himself the least under command. He was still nearly crazed by the catastrophe, and unable to sleep or rest, taking little or no nourishment, frantically going from place to place, he returned to his studio to pace up and down, as if half demented.

Despite the fact that her son seemed scarcely conscious of her existence, and practically ignored her, Mrs. Hammond continued to remain in the apartment. Overwhelmed by remorse and anxiety for her son's health and sanity she could not bring herself to leave, even though she knew at this time her act had driven her son far away from her. A great change was visible in the mother of Jerry. For the first time, possibly, she acquired a vague idea of what her son's work and life meant to him, and her conscience smote her when she realised how he had gone ahead with no encouragement or sympathy from home. On the contrary, she and his father had thrown every obstacle in his way. Like many self-made men, Jerry's father cherished the ambition to perpetuate the business he had successfully built up from what he always called "a shoestring." "I started with just a shoestring," Jerry's father was wont to say, "and what's more, *I* didn't have any education to speak of, yet I beat in the race most of the college bred bunch." However, his parents had had great faith in the change that would come to Jerry after matrimony, and Miss Falconer, being a daughter of Hammond, Sr.'s, partner, the prospects up to this time had not been without hope.

Now, Jerry's mother, away from the somewhat overpowering influence of his father, was seeing a new light. Many a tear she dropped upon Jerry's sketch books, and she suffered the pang of one who has had the opportunity to help one she loved, and who has withheld that sorely needed sympathy. For the first time, too, Jerry's mother appreciated his right to choose his own love. In their anxiety to select for their son a suitable wife, they had overlooked his own wishes in the matter. Now Mrs. Hammond became poignantly aware of his deep love for this strange girl from Japan. She began to feel an unconscious tenderness toward the absent Sunny, and gradually became acquainted with the girl's nature through the medium of the left behind treasures and friends. Sunny's little mongrel dog, the canaries, the gold fish, the nailed up hole where she had fed the mice, her friend the "janitor gentleman," the black elevator boy, the butcher gentleman, the policeman on the beat who had never failed to return Sunny's smiling greeting with a cheery "Top o' the morning to yourself, miss," Hatton—all these revealed more plainly than words could have told that hers was a sensitive and rare nature. In Hatton's case, Mrs. Hammond found a problem upon her hands. The unfortunate valet blamed himself bitterly for Sunny's going. He claimed that he had given his solemn word of honour to Sunny, and had broken that word, when he should have been there: "Like a man, ma'am, hin the place of Mr. 'Ammond, ma'am, to take care of Miss Sunny."

Far from reproving the man, the conscience-stricken Mrs. Hammond wept with him, and asked timid questions about the absent one.

"Miss Sunny was not an hordinary young lady, begging your pardon, ma'am. She was what the French would call distankey. She was sweet and hinnercent as a baby lamb, hutterly hunconscious of her hown beauty hand charm. You wouldn't 'ave believed such hinnocence possible in the present day, ma'am, but Miss Sunny come from a race that's a bit hignorant, ma'am, hand it wasn't her fault that she didn't hunderstan' many of the proper conventions of life. But she was perfectly hinnocent and pure as a lily. Hanyone who looked or spoke to 'er once would've seen that, ma'am. It shone right hout of Miss Sunny's heyes."

"I saw it myself," said Mrs. Hammond, in a low voice.

After a long, sniffling pause, Hatton said:

"Begging your pardon, ma'am, I'm thinking that I don't deserve to work for Mr. 'Ammond any longer, but I 'avent the 'eart to speak to 'im at this time, and if you'll be so kind to hexplain things to 'im, I'll betake myself to some hother abode."

"My good man, I am sure that even Mr. Jerry would not blame you. I am the sole one at fault. I take the full blame. I acknowledge it. I would not have you or anyone else share my guilt, and, Hatton, I *want* to be punished. Your conscience, I am sure, is clear, but it would make us all very happy, and I am sure it would make—Sunny." She spoke the word hesitatingly— "happy, too, if—if—well, if, my good Hatton, you were to turn over a new leaf, and sign the pledge. Drink, I feel sure, is your worst enemy. You must overcome it, Hatton, or it will overcome you."

"Hi will, ma'am. Hi'll do that. If you'll pardon me now, Hi'll step right out and sign the pledge. I know just where to go, if you'll pardon me."

Hatton did know just where to go. He crossed the park to the east side and came to the brightly lighted Salvation Army barracks. A meeting was in progress, and a fiery tongued young woman was exhorting all the sinners of the world to come to glory. Hatton was fascinated by the groans and loud Amens that came from that chorus of human wreckage. Pushing nearer to the front, he came under the penetrating eye of the Salvation captain. She hailed him as a "brother," and there was something so unswervingly pure in her direct gaze that it had the effect of magnetising Hatton.

"Brother," said the Salvation captain, "are you saved?"

"No, ma'am," said the unhappy Hatton, "but begging your pardon, if it haren't hout of horder, Hi'd like to be taking the pledge, ma'am."

"Nothing is out of order where a human soul is at stake," said the woman, smiling in an exalted way. "Lift up your hand, my brother."

Hatton lifted his shaking hand, and, word for word, he repeated the pledge after the Salvation captain. Nor was there one in that room who found aught to laugh at in the words of Hatton.

"Hi promise, with God's 'elp," said Hatton, "to habstain from the use of halcoholic liquors as a beverage, from chewing tobaccer or speaking profane and himpure languidge."

Having thus spoken, Hatton felt a glow of relief and a sense of transfiguration. He experienced, in fact, that hysterical exhilaration that "converts" feel, as if suddenly he were reborn, and had come out of the mud into the clean air. At such moments martyrs, heroes and saints are made. Hatton, the automaton-like valet of the duplex studio, with his "yuman 'ankerings" was afire with a true spiritual fervour. We leave him then marching forth from the barracks with the Salvation Army, his head thrown up, and singing loudly of glory.

On the third day after the disappearance of Sunny, Professor Timothy Barrowes arrived in New York City with the dinornis skeleton of the quaternary period, dug up from the clay of the Red Deer cliffs of Canada. This precious find was duly transported to the Museum of Natural History, where it was set up by the skilled hands of college workmen, who were zealots even as the little man who nagged and adjured them as he had the excavators on the Red Deer River. So absorbed, in fact, was Professor Barrowes by his fascinating employment, that he left his beloved fossil only when the pressing necessity of further funds from his friend and financial agent (Jerry had raised the money to finance the dinornis) necessitated his calling upon Jerry Hammond, who had made no response to his latter telegrams and letters.

Accordingly Professor Barrowes wended his way from the museum to Jerry's studio. Here, enthused and happy over the success of his trip, he failed to notice the abnormal condition of Jerry, whose listless hot hand dropped from his, and whose eye went roving absently above the head of his volubly chattering friend. It was only after the restless and continued pacing of the miserable Jerry and the failure to respond to questions put to him continued for some time, that Professor Barrowes was suddenly apprized that all was not well with his friend. He stopped midway in a long speech in which words like Mesozoic, Triassic and Jurassic prevailed and snapped his glasses suddenly upon his nose. Through these he scrutinised the perturbed and oblivious Jerry scientifically. The glasses were blinked off. Professor Barrowes seized the young man by the arm and stopped him as he started to cross the room for possibly the fiftieth time.

"Come! Come! What is it? What is the trouble, lad?"

Jerry turned his bloodshot eyes upon his old teacher. His unshaven, haggard face, twitching from the effects of his acute nearness to nervous prostration, startled Professor Barrowes. Lack of sleep, refusal of nourishment, the ceaseless search, the agonising fear and anguished longing took their full toll from the unhappy Jerry, but as his glance met the firm one of his friend, a tortured cry broke from his lips.

"Oh, for God's sake, Professor Barrowes, why did you not come when I asked you to? Sunny—*Oh, my God!*"

Professor Barrowes had Jerry's hand gripped closely in his own, and the disjointed story came out at last.

Sunny had come! Sunny had gone! He loved Sunny! He could not live without Sunny—but Sunny had gone! They had turned her out into the streets—his own mother and Miss Falconer.

For the first time, it may be said, since his discovery of the famous fossil of the Red Deer River, Professor Barrowes's mind left his beloved dinornis. He came back solidly to earth, shot back by the calling need of Jerry. Now the man of science was wide awake, and an upheaval was taking place within him. The words of his first telegram to Jerry rattled through his head just then: "The dinornis more important than Sunny." Now as he looked down on the bowed head of the boy for whom he cherished almost a father's love, Professor Barrowes knew that all the dried-up fossils of all the ages were as a handful of worthless dust as compared with this single living girl.

By main force Professor Barrowes made Jerry lie down on that couch, and himself served him the food humbly prepared by his heartbroken mother, who told Jerry's friend with a quivering lip that she felt sure he would not wish to take it from his mother's hands.

There was no going out for Jerry on that night. His protestations fell on deaf ears, and as a further precaution, Professor Barrowes secured possession of the key of the apartment. Only when the professor pointed out to him the fact that a breakdown on his part would mean the cessation of his search would Jerry finally submit to the older man taking his place temporarily. And so, at the telephone, which rang constantly all of that evening, Professor Barrowes took command. A thousand clues were everlastingly turning up. These were turned over to Jinx and Bobs, the former flying from one part of the city and country to another in his big car, and the latter, with an army of newspaper men helping him, and given full license by his paper, influenced by the elder Hammond and Potter. Finally, Professor Barrowes, having given certain instructions to turn telephone calls over to Monty in Bobs' apartment, sat down to Jerry's disordered work table, and, glasses perched on the end of his nose, he sorted out the mail. The afternoon letters still lay unopened, tossed down in despair by Jerry, when he failed to find that characteristic writing that he knew was Sunny's.

But now Professor Barrowes' head had suddenly jerked forward. His chin came out curiously, and his eyes blinked in amazement behind his glasses. He set them on firmer, fiercely, and slowly reread that two-line epistle. The hand holding the paper shook, but the eyes behind the glasses were bright.

"Jerry—come hither, young man!" he growled, his dry old face quivering up with something that looked comically like a smile glaring through threatened tears. "Read that."

Across the table Jerry reached over and took the letter from the famous steel magnate of New York. He read it slowly, dully, and then with a sense as of something breaking in his head and heart. Every word of those two lines sank like balm into his comprehension and consciousness. Then it seemed that a surge of blood rushed through his being, blinding him. The world rocked for Jerry Hammond. He saw a single star gleaming in a firmament that was all black. Down into immeasurable depths of space sank Jerry Hammond.

CHAPTER XV

Sunny, after she left Jerry's apartment, might be likened to a little wounded wild thing, who has trailed off with broken wing. She had never consciously committed a wrong act. Motherless, worse than fatherless, young, innocent, lovely, how should she fare in a land whose ways were as foreign to that from which she had come as if she had been transplanted to a new planet.

As she turned into Sixth Avenue, under the roaring elevated structure, with its overloaded trains, crammed with the home-going workers of New York, she had no sense of direction and no clear purpose in mind. All she felt was that numb sense of pain at her heart and the impulse to get as far away as possible from the man she loved. Swept along by a moving, seething throng that pressed and pushed and shoved and elbowed by her, Sunny had a sick sense of home longing, an inexpressible yearning to escape from all this turmoil and noise, this mad rushing and pushing and panting through life that seemed to spell America. She sensed the fact that she was in the Land of Barbarians, where everyone was racing and leaping and screaming in an hysteria of speed. Noise, noise, incessant noise and movement—that was America! No one stopped to think; no polite words were uttered to the stranger. It was all a chaos, a madhouse, wherein dark figures rushed by like shadows in the night and little children played in the mud of the streets.

The charming, laughing, pretty days in the shelter of the studio of her friend had passed into this nightmare of the Sixth Avenue noise, where all seemed ugly, cruel and sinister. Life in America was not the charming kindly thing Sunny had supposed. Beauty indeed she had brought in her heart with her, and that, though she knew it not, was why she had seen only the beautiful; but now, even for her, it had all changed. She had looked into faces full of hatred and malice; she had listened to words that whipped worse than the lash of Hirata.

As she went along that noisy, crowded avenue, there came, like a breath of spring, a poignant lovely memory of the home she had left. Like a vision, the girl saw wide spaces, little blue houses with pink roofs and the lower floor open to the refreshing breezes of the spring. For it was springtime in Japan just as it was in New York, and Sunny knew that the trees would be freighted with a glorified frost of pink and white blossoms. The wistaria vines would hang in purple glory to peer at their faces in the crystal pools. The fluttering sleeves of the happy picnickers threading through lanes of long slender bamboos. The lotus in the ponds would soon open their white fingers to the sun. Rosy cheeked children would laugh at Sunny and pelt her with flower petals, and she would call back to them, and toss her fragrant petals back.

It was strange as she went along that dirty way that her mind escaped from what was before and on all sides of her, and went out across the sea. She saw no longer the passing throngs. In imagination the girl from Japan looked up a hill slope on which a temple shone. Its peaks were twisted and the tower of the pagoda seemed ablaze with gold. Countless steps led upward to the pagoda, but midway of the steps there was a classic Torrii, in which was a small shrine. Here on a pedestal, smiling down upon the kneeling penitents, Kuonnon, the Goddess of Mercy, stood. To Her now, in the streets of the American City, the girl of Japan sent out her petition.

"Oh, Kuonnon, sweet Lady of Mercy, permit the spirit of my honourable mother to walk with me through these dark and noisy streets."

The shining Goddess of Mercy, trailing her robes among the million stars in the heavens above, surely heard that tiny petition, for certain it is that something warm and comforting swept over the breast of the tired Sunny. We know that faith will "remove mountains." Sunny's faith in her mother's spirit caused her to feel assured that it walked by her side. The Japanese believe that we can think our dead alive, and if we are pure and worthy, we may indeed recall them.

It came to pass, that after many hours, during which she walked from 67th Street to 125th, and from the west to the east side of that avenue, that she stopped before a brightly lighted window, within which cakes and confections were enticingly displayed, and from the cellar of which warm odours of cooking were wafted to the famished girl. Sunny's youth and buoyant health responded to that claim. Her feet, in the unaccustomed American shoes—in Japan she had worn only sandals and clogs—were sore and extremely weary from the long walk, and a sense of intense exhaustion added to that pang of emptiness within.

By the baker's window, therefore, on the dingy Third Avenue of the upper east side, leaned Sunny, staring in hungrily at the food so near and yet so far away. She asked herself in her quaint way:

"What I are now to do? My honourable insides are ask for food."

She answered her own question at once.

"I will ask the advice of first person I meet. He will tell me."

The streets were in a semi-deserted condition, such as follows after the home-going throngs have been tucked away into their respective abodes. There was a cessation of traffic, only the passing of the trains overhead breaking the hush of early night that comes even in the City of New York. It was now fifteen minutes to nine, and Sunny had had nothing to eat since her scant breakfast.

Kuonnon, her mother's spirit, providence—call it what we may—suffered it that the first person whom Sunny was destined to meet should be Katy Clarry, a product of the teeming east side, a shop girl by trade. She was crossing the street, with her few small packages, revealing her pitiful night marketing at adjacent small shops, when Sunny accosted her.

"Aexcuse me. I lig' ask you question, please," said Sunny with timid politeness.

"Uh-h-h?"

Miss Clarry, her grey, clear eye sweeping the face of Sunny in one comprehensive glance that took her "number," stopped short at the curb, and waited for the question.

"I are hungry," said Sunny simply, "and I have no money and no house in which to sleep these night. What I can do?"

"Gee!" Katy's grey eyes flew wider. The girl before her seemed as far from being a beggar as anyone the east side girl had ever seen. Something in the wistful, lovely face looking at her in the dark street tightened that cord that was all mother in the breast of Katy Clarry. After a moment:

"Are you stone broke then? Out of work? You don't look's if you could buck up against tough luck. What you doin' on the streets? You ain't——? No, you ain't. I needn't insult you by askin' that. Where's your home, girl?"

"I got no home," said Sunny, in a very faint voice. A subtle feeling was stealing over the tired Sunny, and the whiteness of her cheeks, the drooping of her eyes, apprized Katy of her condition.

"Say, don't be fallin' whatever you do. You don't want no cop to get 'is hands on you. You come along with me. I ain't got much, but you're welcome to share what I got. I'll stake you till you get a job. Heh! Get a grip on yourself. There! That's better. Hold on to me. I'll put them packages under this arm. We ain't got far to walk. Steady now. We don't want no cop to say we're full, because we ain't."

Katy led the trembling Sunny along the dirty, dingy avenue to one of those melancholy side streets of the upper east side. They came to a house whose sad exterior proclaimed what was within. Here Katy applied her latch key, and in the dark and odorous halls they found their way up four flights of stairs. Katy's room was at the far end of a long bare hall, and its dimensions were little more than the shining kitchenette of the studio apartment.

Katy struck a match, lit a kerosene lamp, and attached to the one half-plugged gas jet a tube at the end of which was a one-burner gas stove. Sunny, sitting helplessly on the bed, was too dazed and weary to hold her position for long, and at Katy's sharp: "Heh, there! lie down," she subsided back upon the bed, sighing with relief as her exhausted body felt the comfort of Katy's hard little bed. From sundry places Katy drew forth a frying pan, a pitcher of water, a tiny kettle and a teapot. She put two knives and forks and spoons on the table, two cracked plates and two cups. She peeled a single potato, and added it to the two frankfurters frying on the pan. She chattered along as she worked, partly to hide her own feelings, and partly to set the girl at her ease. But indeed Sunny was far from feeling an embarrassment such as Katy in her place might have felt. The world is full of two kinds of people; those who serve, and those who are served, and to the latter family Sunny belonged. Not the lazy, wilful parasites of life, but the helpless children, whom we love to care for. Katy, glancing with a maternal eye, ever and anon at the so sad and lovely face upon her pillow was curiously touched and animated with a desire to help her.

"You're dog-tired, ain't you? How long you been out of work? I always feel more tired when I'm out o' work and looking for a job, than when I got one, though it ain't my idea of a rest exactly to stand on your feet all day long shoving out things you can't afford to have yourself to folks who mostly just want to look 'em over. Some of them shoppers love to come in just about closin' hour. They should worry whether the girl behind the counter gets extra pay for overtime or if she's suffering from female weaknesses or not. Of course, if I get into one of them big stores downtown, I can give a customer the laugh when the dingdong sounds for closin', but you can't do no such thing in Harlem. We're still in the pioneer stage up here. I expect you're more used to the Fifth Avenue joints. You look it, but, say, I never got a look in at one of them jobs. They favour educated girls, and I ain't packed with learning, I'm telling the world."

Sunny said:

"You loog good to me,"—a favourite expression of Jerry's, and something in her accent and the earnestness with which she said it warmed Katy, who laughed and said:

"Oh, go on. I ain't much on looks neither. There, now. Draw up. All—l-ler *ready*! Dinner is served. Stay where you are on the bed. Drop your feet over. I ain't got but the one chair, and I'll have it meself, thank you, don't mention it."

Katy pushed the table beside the bed, drew her own chair to the other side, set the kettle on the jet which the frying pan had released and proudly surveyed her labour.

"Not much, but looks pretty good to me. If there's one thing I love it is a hot dog."

She put on Sunny's plate the largest of the two frankfurters and three-quarters of the potato, cut her a generous slice of bread and poured most of the gravy on her plate, saying:

"I always say sausage gravy beats anything in the butter line. Tea'll be done in a minute, dearie. Ain't got but one burner. Gee! I wisht I had one of them two deckers that you can cook a whole meal at once with. Ever seen 'em? How's your dog?"

"Dog?"

"Frankfurter—weeny, or in polite speech, sausage, dearie."

"How it is good," said Sunny with simple eloquence. "I thang you how much."

"Don't mention it. You're welcome. You'd do the same for me if I was busted. I always say one working girl should stake the other when the other is out of work and broke. There's unity in strength," quoted Katy with conviction. "Have some more—do! Dip your bread in the gravy. Pretty good, ain't it, if I do say it who shouldn't."

"It mos' nices' food I are ever taste," declared Sunny earnestly.

While the tea was going into the cups:

"My name's Katy Clarry. What's yours?" asked Katy, a sense of well-being and good humour toward the world flooding her warm being.

"Sunny."

"Sunny! That's a queer name. Gee! ain't it pretty? What's your other name?"

"Sindicutt."

"Sounds kind o' foreign. What are you, anyway? You ain't American—at least you don't look it or talk it, though heaven knows anything and everything calls itself American to-day," said the native-born American girl with scorn. "Meaning no offence, you understand, but—well—you just don't look like the rest of us. You ain't a Dago or a Sheeny. I can see that, and you ain't a Hun neither. Are you a Frenchy? You got queer kind of eyes—meaning no offence, for personally I think them lovely, I really do. I seen actresses with no better eyes than you got."

Katy shot her questions at Sunny, without waiting for an answer. Sunny smiled sadly.

"Katy, I are sawry thad I am not be American girl. I are born ad Japan——"

"*You* ain't no Chink. You can't tell me no such thing as that. I wasn't born yesterday. What are you, anyway? Where do you come from? Are you a royal princess in disguise?"

The latter question was put jocularly, but Katy in her imaginative way was beginning to question whether her guest might not in fact be some such personage. An ardent reader of the yellow press, by inheritance a romantic dreamer, in happier circumstances Katy might have made a place for herself in the artistic world. Her sordid life had been ever glorified by her extravagant dreams in which she moved as a princess in a realm where princes and lord and kings and dukes abounded.

"No, I are not princess," said Sunny sadly. "I not all Japanese, Katy, jos liddle bit. Me? I got three kind of blood on my insides. I sawry thad my ancestors put them there. I are Japanese and Russian and American."

"Gee! You're what we call a mongrel. Meaning no offence. You can't help yourself. Personally I stand up first for the home-made American article but I ain't got no prejudice against no one. And anyway, you can *grow* into an American if you want to. Now we women have got the francheese, we got the right to vote and be nachelised too if we want to. So even if you have a yellow streak in you—and looking at you, I'd say it was gold moren't yellow—you needn't tell no one about it. No one'll be the wiser. You can trust me not to open my mouth to a living soul about it. What you've confided in me about being partly Chink is just as if you had put the inflammation in a tomb. And it ain't going to make the least bit of difference between us. Try one of them Uneeda crackers. Sop it in your tea now you're done with your gravy. Pretty good, ain't it? I'll say it is."

"Katy, to-night I are going to tell you some things about me, bi-cause I know you are my good frien' now forever. I lig' your kind eye, Katy."

"Go on! You're kiddin' me, Sunny. If I had eyes like yours, it'd be a different matter. But I'm stuck on the idea of having you for a friend just the same. I ain't had a chum since I don't know when. If you knew what them girls was like in Bamberger's—well, I'm not talkin' about no one behind their backs, but, say—Sunny, I could tell you a thing or two'd make your hair stand on end. And as for tellin' me about your own past, say if you'll tell me yours, I'll tell you mine. I always say that every girl has some tradgedy or other in her life. Mine began on the lower east side. I graduated up here, Sunny. It ain't nothing to brag about, but it's heaven compared with what's downtown. I used to live in that gutter part of the town where God's good air is even begrudged you, and where all the dirty forriners and chinks—meanin' no offence, dearie, and I'll say for the Chinks, that compared with some of them Russian Jews—Gee! you're Russian too, ain't you, but I don't mean no offence! Take it from me, Sunny, some of them east side forriners—I'll call them just that to avoid givin' offence—are just exactly like lice, and the smells down there—Gee! the stock yards is a flower garden compared with it. Well, we come over—my folks did—I was born there—I'm a real American, Sunny. Look me over. It won't hurt your eyes none. My folks come over from Ireland. My mother often told me that they thought the streets of New York were just running with gold, before they come out. That simple they were, Sunny. But the gold was nothing but plain, rotten dust. It got into the lungs and the spine of them all. Father went first. Then mother. Lord only knows how they got it—doctor said it was from the streets, germs that someone maybe dumped out and come flyin' up into our place that was the only clean spot in the tenement house, I'll say that for my mother. There was two kids left besides me. I was the oldes' and not much on age at that, but I got me a job chasin' around for a millinery shop, and I did my best by the kids when I got home nights; but the cards was all stacked against me, Sunny, and when that infantile parallysus come on the city, the first to be took was my k-kid brother, and me li-little s-sister she come down with it too and—Ah-h-h-h!"

Katy's head went down on the table, and she sobbed tempestuously. Sunny, unable to speak the words of comfort that welled up in her heart, could only put her arms around Katy, and mingle her tears with hers. Katy removed a handkerchief from the top of her waist, dabbed her eyes fiercely, shared the little ball with Sunny, and then thrust it down the neck of her waist again. Bravely she smiled at Sunny again.

"There yoh got the story of the Clarry's of the east side of New York, late of Limerick, Ireland. You can't beat it for—for tradgedy, now can you? So spiel away at your own story, Sunny. I'm thinkin' you'll have a hard time handin' me out a worse one than me own. Don't spare me, kid. I'm braced for anything in this r-rotten world."

CHAPTER XVI

It was well for Sunny that her new friend was endowed with a generous and belligerent nature. Having secured for Sunny a position at the Bamberger Emporium, Katy's loyalty to her friend was not dampened when on the third day Sunny was summarily discharged. Hands on hips, Katy flew furiously to her brother's defence, and for the benefit of her brother and sister workers she relieved herself loudly of all her pent-up rage of the months. In true Union style, Katy marched out with Sunny. The excuse for discharging Sunny was that she did not write well enough to fill out the sales slips properly. Nasty as the true reason was, there is no occasion to set forth the details here.

Suffice it to say that the two girls, both rosy from excitement and wrath, arm and arm marched independently forth from the Emporium, Katy loudly asserting that she would sue for her half week's pay, and Sunny anxiously drawing her along, her breath coming and going with the fright she had had.

"Gee!" snorted Katy, as they turned into the street on which was the dingy house in which they lived, "it did my soul good to dump its garbage on that pie-faced, soapy-eyed monk. You don't know what I been through since I worked for them people. You done me a good turn this mornin' when you let out that scream. I'd been expecting something like that ever since he dirtied you with his eyes. That's why I was hangin' around the office, in spite of the ribbon sales, when you went in. Well, here we are!"

Here they were indeed, back in the small ugly room of that fourth floor, sitting, the one on the ricketty chair, and the other on the side of the hard bed. But the eyes of youth are veiled in sun and rose. They see nor feel not the filth of the world. Sunny and Katy, out of a job, with scarcely enough money between them to keep body and soul together, were yet able to laugh at each other and exchange jokes over the position in which they found themselves.

After they had "chewed the rag," as Katy expressively termed it, for awhile, that brisk young person removed her hat, rolled up her sleeves, and declared she would do the "family wash."

"It's too late now," said Katy, "to job hunt this morning. So I'll do the wash, and you waltz over across the street and do the marketin'. Here's ten cents, and get a wiggle on you, because it's 10.30 now, and I got a plan for us two. I'll tell you what it is. There ain't no hurry. Just wait a bit, dearie. First we'll have a bite to eat, though I'm not hungry myself. I always say, though, you can land a job better on a full than a empty stomach. Well, lunch packed away in us, little you and me trots downtown—not to no 125th Street, mind you, but downtown, to Fifth Avenoo, where the swell shops are, do you get me? I'd a done this long ago, for they say it's as easy to land on Fifth Avenoo as it is on Third. It's like goods, Sunny. The real silk is cheaper than the fake stuff, because it lasts longer and is wider, but if one ain't got the capital to invest in it in the first place, why you just have to make the best of the imitation cheese. If I could of dolled myself up like them girls that hold down the jobs on Fifth Avenoo, say, you can take it from me, I'd a made some of them henna-haired ladies look like thirty cents. Now *you* got the looks, and you got the clothes too. That suit you're wearin' don't look like no million dollars, but it's got a kick to it just the same. The goods is real. I been lookin' at it. Where'd you get it?"

"I get that suit ad Japan, Katy."

"Japan! What are you givin' us? You can't tell me no Chink ever made a suit like that."

Sunny nodded vigorously.

"Yes, Katy, Japanese tailor gentleman make thad suit. He copy it from American suit just same on lady at hotel, and he tell me that he are just like twin suits."

"I take off my hat to that Chink, though I always have heard they was great on copying. However, it's unmaterial who made it, and it don't detract from its looks, and no one will be the wiser that a Chink tailor made it. You can trust me not to open my mouth. The main thing is that that suit and your face—and everything about you is going to make a hit on Fifth Avenoo. You see how Bamberger fell for you at the drop, and you could be there still and have the best goin' if you was like some ladies I know, though I'm not mentionin' no names. I'm not that kind, Sunny. Now, here's my scheme, and see if you can beat it. Your face and suit'll land the jobs for us. My brains'll hold 'em for us. Do you get me? You'll accept a position—you don't say job down there—only on condition that they take your friend—that's me—too. Then together we prove the truth of 'Unity being strength.' We'll hang together. Said Lincoln" (Katy raised her head with true solemnity): "'Together we rise, divided we fall!' Shake on that, Sunny." Shake they did. "Now you skedaddle off for that meat. Ask for dog. It goes farther and is fillin'. Give the butcher the soft look, and he'll give you your money's worth—maybe throw in an extra dog for luck."

At the butcher shop, Sunny, when her turn came, favoured the plump gentleman behind the counter to such an engaging smile that he hurriedly glanced about him to see if the female part of his establishment were around. The coast clear, he returned the smile with interest. Leaning gracefully upon the long bloody butcher knife in one hand, the other toying with a juicy sirloin, he solicited the patronage of the smiling Sunny. She put her ten cents down, and continuing the smile, said:

"Please you give me plenty dog meat for those money."

"Surest thing," said the flattered butcher. "I got a pile just waitin' for a customer like you."

He disappeared into a hole in the floor, and returned up the ladder shortly, bearing an extremely large package, which he handed across to the surprised and overjoyed Sunny, who cried:

"Ho! I are thang you. How you are kind. I thang you very moach. Good-aday!"

It so happened that when Sunny had come out of the house upon that momentous marketing trip a pimply-faced youth was lolling against the railing of the house next door. His dress and general appearance made him conspicuous in that street of mean and poverty-stricken houses, for he wore the latest thing in short pinch-back coats, tight trousers raised well above silk-clad ankles, pointed and polished tan shoes, a green tweed hat and a cane and cigarette loosely hung in a loose mouth. A harmless enough looking specimen of the male family at first sight, yet one at which the sophisticated members of the same sex would give a keen glance and then turn away with a scowl of aversion and rage. Society has classified this type of parasite inadequately as "Cadet," but the neighbourhood in which he thrives designates him with one ugly and expressive term.

As Sunny came out of the house and ran lightly across the street, the youth wagged his cigarette from the corner of one side of his mouth to the other, squinted appraisingly at the hurrying girl, and then followed her across the street. Through the opened door of the kosher butcher shop, he heard the transaction, and noted the joy of Sunny as the great package was transferred to her arms. As she came out of the shop, hurrying to bear the good news to Katy, she was stopped at the curb by the man, his hat gracefully raised, and a most ingratiating smile twisting his evil face into a semblance of what might have appeared attractive to an ignorant and weak minded girl.

"I beg your pardon, Miss—er—Levine. I believe I met you at a friend's house."

"You are mistake," said Sunny. "My name are not those. Good-a-day!"

He continued to walk by her side, murmuring an apology for the mistake, and presently as if just discovering the package she carried, he affected concern.

"Allow me to carry that for you. It's entirely too heavy for such pretty little arms as yours."

"Thang you. I lig' better carry him myself," said Sunny, holding tightly to her precious package.

Still the pimpled faced young man persisted at her side, and as they reached the curb, his hand at her elbow, he assisted her to the sidewalk. Standing at the foot of the front steps, he practically barred her way.

"You live here?"

"Yes, I do so."

"I believe I know Mrs. Munson, the lady that keeps this house. Relative of yours?"

"No, I are got no relative."

"All alone here?"

"No, I got frien' live wiz me. Aexcuse me. I are in hoarry eat my dinner."

"I wonder if I know your friend. What is his name?"

"His name are Katy."

"Ah, don't hurry. I believe, now I think of it, I know Katy. What's the matter with your comin' along and havin' dinner with me."

"Thang you. My frien' are expect me eat those dinner with her."

"That's all right. I have a friend too. Bring Katy along, and we'll all go off for a blowout. What do you say? A sweet little girl like you don't need to be eatin' dog meat. I know a swell place where we can get the best kind of eats, a bit of booze to wash it down and music and dancing enough to make you dizzy. What do you say?"

He smiled at Sunny in what he thought was an irresistible and killing way. It revealed three decayed teeth in front, and brought his shifty eyes into full focus upon the shrinking girl.

"I go ask my frien'," she said hurriedly. "Aexcuse me now. You are stand ad my way."

He moved unwillingly to let her pass.

"Surest thing. More the merrier. Let's go up and get Katy. What floor you on?"

"I bring Katy down," said Sunny breathlessly, and running by the pasty faced youth, she opened the door, and closed it quickly behind her, shooting the lock closed. She ran up the stairs, as if pursued, and burst breathlessly into the little room where Katy was singing a ditty composed to another of her name, and pasting her lately washed handkerchiefs upon the window pane and mirror.

"Beautiful K-Katy—luvully Katy!You're the only one that ever I adore, Wh-en the moon shines, on the cow shed,I'll be w-waiting at the k-k-k-kitchen door!"

sang the light-hearted and valiant Katy Clarry.

"Oh, Katy," cried Sunny breathlessly. "Here are those dog." She laid the huge package before the amazed and incredulous Katy.

"For the love of Mike! Did Schmidt sell you a whole cow?"

Katy tore the wrappings aside, and revealed the contents of the package. An assortment of bones of all sizes, large and small, a few pieces of malodorous meat, livers, lights and guts, and the insides of sundry chickens. Katy sat down hard, exclaiming:

"Good night! What did you ask for?"

"I ask him for dog meat," excitedly and indignantly declared Sunny.

"You got it! You poor simp. Heaven help you. Never mind, there's no need now of crying over spilled beans. It's too late now to change, so here's where we kiss our lunch a long and last farewell, and do some hustling downtown."

"Oh, Katy, I am thad sorry!" cried Sunny tragically.

"It's all right, dearie. Don't you worry. You can't help being ignorant. I ain't hungry myself anyway, and you're welcome to the cracker there. That'll do till we get back, and then, why, I believe we can boil some of them bones and get a good soup. I always say soup is just as fillin' as anything else, especially if you put a onion in it, and have a bit of bread to sop it up with, and I got the onion all right. So cheer up, we'll soon be dead and the worst is yet to come."

"Katy, there are a gentleman down on those street, who are want give us nize dinner to eat, with music and some danze. Me? I am not care for those music, but I lig' eat those dinner, and I lig' also thad you eat him."

"Gentleman, huh?" Katy's head cocked alertly.

"Yes, he speak at me on the street, and he say he take me and my frien' out to nize dinner. He are wait in those street now."

Katy went to the window, leaned far out, saw the man on the street, and drew swiftly in, her face turning first white, then red.

"Sunny, ain't you got any better sense than speak to a man on the street?"

"Ho, Katy, I din nod speag ad those man," declared Sunny indignantly. "He speag ad me, and I do nod lig' hees eye. I do nod lig' hees mout', nor none of hees face, but I speag perlite bi-cause he are ask me eat those dinner."

"Well, you poor little simp, let me tell you who *that* is. He's the dirtiest swine in Harlem. You're muddied if he looks at you. He's—he's—I can't tell you what he is, because you're so ignorunt you wouldn't understand. You and me go out with the likes of him! Sa-ay, I'd rather duck into a sewer. I'd come out cleaner, believe me. Now watch how little K-k-k-katy treats that kind of dirt."

She transferred the more decayed of the meat and bones from the package to the pail of water which had recently served for her "family wash." This she elevated to the window, put her head out, and as if sweetly to signal the waiting one below, she called:

"Hi-yi-yi-yi—i-i!" and as the man below looked up expectantly, she gave him the full benefit of the pail's contents in his upturned face.

The sight of the drenched, spluttering and foully swearing rat on the street below struck the funny side of the two young girls. Clinging together, they burst into laughter, holding their sides, and with their young heads tossed back; but their laughter had an element of hysteria to it, and when at last they stopped, and the stream of profanity from below continued to pour into the room, Katy soberly closed the window. For a while they stared at each other in a scared silence. Then Katy, squaring her shoulders, belligerently said:

"Well, we should worry over that one."

Sunny was standing now by the bureau. A very thoughtful expression had come to Sunny's face, and she opened the top drawer and drew out her little package.

"Katy," she said softly, "here are some little thing ad these package, which mebbe it goin' to help us."

"Say, I been wonderin' what you got in that parcel ever since you been here. I'd a asked you, but as you didn't volunteer no inflamation, I was too much of a lady to press it, and I'm telling the world, I'd not open no package the first time myself, without knowin' what was in it, especially as that one looks kind of mysteriees and foreign looking. I heard about a lady named Pandora something and when she come to open a box she hadn't no right to open, it turned into smoke and she couldn't get it back to where she wanted it to go. What you got there, dearie, if it ain't being too personal to ask? I'll bet you got gold and diamonds hidden away somewhere."

Sunny was picking at the red silk cord. Lovingly she unwrapped the Japanese paper. The touch of her fingers on her mother's things was a caress and had all the reverence that the Japanese child pays in tribute to a departed parent.

"These honourable things belong my mother," said Sunny gently. "She have give them to me when she know she got die. See, Katy, this are kakemona. It very old, mebbe one tousan' year ole. It belong at grade Prince of Satsuma. Thas my mother ancestor. This kakemona, it are so ole as those ancestor," said Sunny reverently.

"Old! Gee, I should say it is. Looks as if it belonged in a tomb. You couldn't hock nothing like that, dearie, meanin' no offence. What else you got?"

"The poor simp!" said Katy to herself, as Sunny drew forth her mother's veil. In the gardens of the House of a Thousand Joys the face of the dancer behind the shimmering veil had aroused the enthusiasm of her admirers. Now Katy bit off the words that were about to explain to Sunny that in her opinion a better veil could be had at Dacy's for ninety-eight cents. All she said, however, was:

"You better keep the veil, Sunny. I know how one feels about a mother's old duds. I got a pair of shoes of my mother's that nothing could buy from me, though they ain't much to look at; but I know how you feel about them things, dearie."

"This," said Sunny, with shining eyes, "are my mother's fan. See, Katy, Takamushi, a grade poet ad Japan, are ride two poem on thad fan and present him to my mother. Thad is grade treasure. I do nod lig' to sell those fan."

"I wouldn't. You just keep it, dearie. We ain't so stone broke that you have to sell your mother's fan."

"These are flower that my mother wear ad her hair when she danze, Katy."

The big artificial poppies that once had flashed up on either side of the dancer's lovely face, Sunny now pressed against her cheek.

"Ain't they pretty?" said Katy, pretending an enthusiasm she did not feel. "You could trim a hat with them if flowers was in fashion this year, but they ain't, dearie. The latest thing is naked hats, sailors, like you got, or treecornes, with nothing on them except the lines. What's that you got there, Sunny?"

"That are a letter, Katy. My mother gave me those letter. She say that some day mebbe I are need some frien'. Then I must put those letter at post office box, or I must take those letter in my hand to thad man it are write to. He are frien' to me, my mother have said."

Katy grabbed the letter, disbelieving her eyes when she read the name inscribed in the thin Japanese hand. It was addressed both in English and Japanese, and the name was, Stephen Holt Wainwright, 27 Broadway, New York City.

"Someone hold me up," cried Katy. "I'm about to faint dead away."

"Oh, Katy, do not be dead away! Oh, Katy, do not do those faint. Here are those cracker. I am not so hungry as you."

"My Lord! You poor ignorunt little simp, don't you reckernise when a fellow is fainting with pure unadulterated joy? How long have you had that letter?"

"Four year now," said Sunny sadly, thinking of the day when her mother had placed it in her hand, and of the look on the face of that mother.

"Why did you never mail it?"

"I was await, Katy. I are not need help. I have four and five good frien' to me then, and I do not need nuther one; but now I are beggar again. I nod got those frien's no more. I need those other one."

"Were you ever a *beggar*, Sunny?"

"Oh, yes, Katy, some time my mother and I we beg for something eat at Japan. Thad is no disgrace. The gods love those beggar jos' same rich man, and when he go on long journey to those Meido, mebbe rich man go behind those beggar. I are hear thad at Japan."

"Do you know who this letter is addressed to, dearie?"

"No, Katy, I cannot read so big a name. My mother say he will be frien' to me always."

"Sunny, I pity you for your ignorunce, but I don't hold it against you. You was born that way. Why, a child could read that name. Goodness knows I never got beyond the Third Grade, yet I *hope* I'm able to read that. It says as plain as the nose on your face, Sunny: Stephen Holt Wainwright. Now that's the name of one of the biggest guns in the country. He's a U. S. senator, or was and is, and he's so rich that he has to hire twenty or fifty cashiers to count his income that rolls in upon him from his vast estates. If you weren't so ignorunt, Sunny, you'd a read about him in the *Journal*. Gee! his picture's in nearly every day, and pictures of his luxurious home and yacht and horses and wife, who's one of the big nobs in this suffrage scare. They call him 'The Man of Steel,' because he owns most of the steel in the world, and because he's got a mug—a face—on him like a steel trap. That's what I've heard and read, though I've never met the gentleman. I expect to, however, very soon, seeing he's a friend of yours. And now, lovey, don't waste no more tears over that other bunch of ginks, because this Senator Wainwright has got them all beat in the Marathon."

"Katy, this letter are written by my mother ad the Japanese language. Mebbe those Sen—a—tor kinnod read them. What I shall do?"

"What you shall do, baby mine? Did you think I was goin' to let precious freight like that go into any post box. Perish the idea, lovey. You and me are going to waltz downtown to 27 Broadway, and we ain't going to do no walking what's more. The Subway for little us. I'm gambling on Mr. Senator passing along a job to friends of his friends. Get your hat on now, and don't answer back neither."

On the way downstairs she gave a final stern order to Sunny.

"Hold your hat pin in your hand as we come out. If his nibs so much as opens his face to you, jab him in the eye. I'll take care of the rest of him."

Thus bravely armed, the two small warriors issued forth, the general marshalling her army of one, with an elevated chin and nose and an eye that scorched from head to foot the craven looking object waiting for them on the street.

"Come along, dearie. Be careful you don't get soiled as we pass."

Laughing merrily, the two girls, with music in their souls, danced up the street, their empty stomachs and their lost jobs forgotten. When they reached the Subway, Katy seized Sunny's hand, and they raced down the steps just as the South Ferry train pulled in.

CHAPTER XVII

That was a long and exciting ride for Sunny. Above the roar of the rushing train Katy shouted in her ear. Perfectly at home in the Subway, Katy did not let a little thing like mere noise deter the steady flow of her tongue. The gist of her remarks came always back to what Sunny was to do when they arrived at 27 Broadway; how she was to look; how speak. She was to bear in mind that she was going into the presence of American royalty, and she was to be neither too fresh nor yet too humble. Americans, high and low, so Katy averred, liked folks that had a kick to them, but not too much of a kick.

Sunny was to find out whether at some time or other in the past, Senator Wainwright had not put himself under deep obligations to some member of Sunny's family. Perhaps some of her relatives might have saved the life of this senator. Even Chinks were occasionally heroes, Katy had heard. It might be, on the other hand, said Katy, that Sunny's mother had something "on" the senator. So much the better. Katy had no objection, so she said, to the use of a bit of refined ladylike blackmail, for "the end justifies the means," said Katy, quoting, so she said, from Lincoln, the source of all her aphorisms. Anyway, the long and short of it was, said Katy, that Sunny was on no account to get cold feet. She was to enter the presence of the mighty man with dignity and coolness. "Keep your nerve whatever you do," urged Katy. Then once eye to eye with the man of power, she was to ask—it was possible, she might even be able to demand—certain favours.

"Ask and it shall be given to you. Shut your mouth and it'll be taken away. That's how things go in this old world," said Katy.

Sunny was to make application in both their names. If there were no vacancies in the senator's office, then she would delicately suggest that the senator could make such a vacancy. Such things were done within Katy's own experience.

Katy had no difficulty in locating the monstrous office building, and she led Sunny along to the elevator with the experienced air of one used to ascending skyward in the crowded cars. Sunny held tight to her arm as they made the breathless ascent. There was no need to ask direction on the 35th floor, since the Wainwright Structural Steel Company occupied the entire floor.

It was noon hour, and Katy and Sunny followed several girls returning from lunch through the main entrance of the offices.

A girl at a desk in the reception hall stopped them from penetrating farther into the offices by calling out:

"No admission there. Who do you want to see? Name, please."

Katy swung around on her heel, and recognising a kindred spirit in the girl at the desk, she favoured her with an equally haughty and glassy stare. Then in a very superior voice, Katy replied:

"We are friends of the Senator. Kindly announce us, if you please."

A grin slipped over the face of the maiden at the desk, and she shoved a pad of paper toward Katy.

Opposite the word "Name" on the pad, Katy wrote, "Miss Sindicutt." Opposite the word: "Business" she wrote "Private and personal and intimate."

The girl at the desk glanced amusedly at the pad, tore the first sheet off, pushed a button which summoned an office boy, to whom she handed the slip of paper. With one eye turned appraisingly upon the girls, he went off backwards, whistling, and disappeared through the little swinging gate that opened apparently into the great offices beyond.

"I beg your pardon?" said Katy to the girl at the desk.

"I didn't say nothing," returned the surprised maiden.

"I thought you said 'Be seated.' I will, thank you. Don't mention it," and Katy grinned with malicious politeness on the discomfited young person, who patted her coiffure with assumed disdain.

Katy meanwhile disposed herself on the long bench, drew Sunny down beside her, and proceeded to scrutinise and comment on all passers through the main reception hall into the offices within. Once in a while she resumed her injunctions to Sunny, as:

"Now don't be gettin' cold feet whatever you do. There ain't nothing to be afraid of. A cat may look at a king, him being the king and you the cat. No offence, dearie. Ha, ha, ha! That's just my way of speaking. Say, Sunny, would you look at her nibs at the desk there. Gee! ain't that a job? Some snap, I'll say. Nothin' to do, but give everyone the once over, push a button and send a boy to carry in your names. Say, if you're a true friend of mine, you'll land me that job. It'd suit me down to a double Tee."

"Katy, I goin' try get you bes' job ad these place. I am not so smart like you, Katy———"

"Oh, well, you can't help that, dearie, and you got the face all right."

- 120 -

"Face is no matter. My mother are tell me many time, it is those heart that matter."

"*Sounds* all right, and I ain't questionin' your mother's opinion, Sunny, but you take it from me, you can go a darn sight further in this old world with a face than a heart."

A man had come into the reception room from the main entrance. He started to cross the room directly to the little swinging door, then stopped to speak to a clerk at a wicket window. Something about the sternness of his look, an air savouring almost of austerity aroused the imp in Katy.

"Well, look who's here," she whispered behind her hand to Sunny. "Now watch little K-k-katy."

As the man turned from the window, and proceeded toward the door, Katy shot out her foot, and the man abstractedly stumbled against it. He looked down at the girl, impudently staring him out of countenance, and frowned at her exaggerated:

"I *beg* your pardon!"

Then his glance turning irritably from Katy, rested upon Sunny's slightly shocked face? He stopped abruptly, standing perfectly still for a moment, staring down at the girl. Then with a muttered apology, Senator Wainwright turned and went swiftly through the swinging door.

"Well, of *all* the nerve!" said Katy. Then to the girl at the desk:

"Who was his nibs?"

"Why, your friend, of course. I'm surprised you didn't recognise him," returned the girl sweetly.

"Him—Senator Wainwright."

"The papers sometimes call him 'The Man of Steel,' but of course, intimate friends like you and your friend there probably call him by a nickname."

"Sure we do," returned Katy brazenly. "I call him 'Sen-Sen' for short. I'd a known him in an instant with his hat off."

"I want to know!" gibed the girl at the desk.

The boy had returned, and thrusting his head over the short gate sang out:

"This way, please, la-adies!"

Katy and Sunny followed the boy across an office where many girls and men were working at desks. The click of a hundred typewriters, and the voices dictating into dictagraphs and to books impressed Katy, but with her head up she swung along behind the boy. At a door marked "Miss Hollowell, Private," the boy knocked. A voice within bade him "Come," and the two girls were admitted.

Miss Hollowell, a clear-eyed young woman of the clean-cut modern type of the efficient woman executive, looked up from her work and favoured them with a pleasant smile.

"What can I do for you?" The question was directed at Katy, but her trained eye went from Katy to Sunny, and there remained in speculative inquiry.

"We have come to call upon the Senator," said Katy, "on important and private business."

Katy was gripping to that something she called her "nerve," but her manner to Miss Hollowell had lost the gibing patronising quality she had affected to the girl at the door. Acute street gamin, as was Katy, she had that unerring gift of sizing up human nature at a glance, a gift not unsimilar in fact to that possessed by the secretary of Senator Wainwright.

Miss Hollowell smiled indulgently at Katy's words.

"*I* see. Well now, I'll speak for Mr. Wainwright. What can we do for you?"

"Nothing. *You* can't do nothing," said Katy. She was not to be beguiled by the smile of this superior young person. "My friend here—meet Miss Sindicutt—has a personal letter for Senator Wainwright, and she's takin' my advice not to let it out of her hands into any but his."

"I'm awfully sorry, because Mr. Wainwright is very busy, and can't possibly see you. I believe I will answer the purpose as well. I'm Mr. Wainwright's secretary."

"We don't want to speak to no secretary," said Katy. "I always say: 'Go to the top. Slide down if you must. You can't slide up.'"

Miss Hollowell laughed.

"Oh, very well then. Perhaps some other time, but we're especially busy to-day, so I'm going to ask you to excuse us. *Good*-day."

She turned back to the papers on her desk, her pencil poised above a sheet of estimates.

Katy pushed Sunny forward, and in dumb show signified that she should speak. Miss Hollowell glanced up and regarded the girl with singular attention. Something in the expression, something in the back of the secretary's mind that concerned Japan, which this strange girl had now mentioned caused her to wait quietly for her to finish the sentence. Sunny held out the letter, and Miss Hollowell saw that fine script upon the envelope, with the Japanese letters down the side.

"This are a letter from Japan," said Sunny. "If you please I will lig' to give those to Sen—Thad is so big a name for me to say." The last was spoken apologetically and brought a sympathetic smile from Miss Hollowell.

"Can't I read it? I'm sure I can give you what information you want as well as Mr. Wainwright can."

"It are wrote in Japanese," said Sunny. "You cannot read that same. *Please* you let me take it to thad gentleman."

Miss Hollowell, with a smile, arose at that plea. She crossed the room and tapped on the door bearing the Senator's name.

Even in a city where offices of the New York magnates are sometimes as sumptuously furnished as drawing rooms, the great room of Senator Wainwright was distinctive. The floor was strewn with priceless Persian and Chinese rugs, which harmonised with the remarkable walls, panelled half way up with mahogany, the upper part of which was hung with masterpieces of the American painters, whose work the steel magnate especially favoured. Stephen Wainwright was seated at a big mahogany desk table, that was at the far end of the room, between the great windows, which gave upon a magnificent view of the Hudson River and part of the Harbor. He was not working. His elbows on the desk, he seemed to be staring out before him in a mood of strange abstraction. His face, somewhat stony in expression, with straight grey eyes that had a curious trick when turned on one of seeming to pin themselves in an appraising stare, his iron grey hair and the grey suit which he invariably wore had given him the name of "The Man of Steel." Miss Hollowell, with her slightly professional smile, laid the slip of paper on the desk before him.

"A Miss Sindicutt. She has a letter for you—a letter from Japan she says. She wishes to deliver it in person."

At the word "Japan" he came slightly out of his abstraction, stared at the slip of paper, and shook his head.

"Don't know the name."

"Yes, I knew you didn't; but, still, I believe I'd see her if I were you."

"Very well. Send her in."

Miss Hollowell at the door nodded brightly to Sunny, but stayed Katy, who triumphantly was pushing forward.

"Sorry, but Mr. Wainwright will see just Miss Sindicutt."

Sunny went in alone. She crossed the room hesitantly and stood by the desk of the steel magnate, waiting for him to speak to her. He remained unmoving, half turned about in his seat, staring steadily at the girl before him. If a ghost had arisen suddenly in his path, Senator Wainwright could not have felt a greater agitation. After a long pause, he found his voice, murmuring:

"I beg your pardon. Be seated, please."

Sunny took the chair opposite him. Their glances met and remained for a long moment locked. Then the man tried to speak lightly:

"You wished to see me. What can I do for you?"

Sunny extended the letter. When he took it from her hand, his face came somewhat nearer to hers, and the closer he saw that young girl's face, the greater grew his agitation.

"What is your name?" he demanded abruptly.

"Sunny," said the girl simply, little dreaming that she was speaking the name that the man before her had himself invented for her seventeen and a half years before.

The word touched some electrical cord within him. He started violently forward in his seat, half arising, and the letter in his hand dropped on the table before him face up. A moment of gigantic self-control, and then with fingers that shook, Stephen Wainwright slipped the envelope open. The words swam before him, but not till they were indelibly printed upon the man's conscience-stricken heart. Through blurred vision he read the message from the dead to the living.

"On this sixth day of the Season of Little Plenty. A thousand years of joy. It is your honourable daughter, who knows not your name, who brings or sends to you this my letter. I go upon the long journey to the Meido. I send my child to him through whom she has her life. Sayonara. Haru-no."

For a long, long time the man sat with his two hands gripped before him on the desk, steadily looking at the girl before him, devouring every feature of the well-remembered face of the child he had always loved. It seemed to him that she had changed not at all. His little Sunny of those charming days of his youth had that same crystal look of supreme innocence, a quality of refinement, a fragrance of race that seemed to reach back to some old ancestry, and put its magic print upon the exquisite young face. He felt he must have been blind not to have recognised his own child the instant his eye had fallen upon her. He knew now what that warm rush of emotion had meant when he had looked at her in that outer office. It was the intuitive instinct that his own child was near—the only child he had ever had. By exercising all the self-control that he could command, he was at last able to speak her name, huskily.

"Sunny, don't you remember me?"

Like her father, Sunny was addicted to moments of abstraction. She had allowed her gaze to wander through the window to the harbour below, where she could see the great ships at their moorings. It made her think of the one she had come to America on, and the one on which Jerry had sailed away from Japan. Painfully, wistfully, she brought her gaze back to her father's face. At his question she essayed a little propitiating smile.

"Mebbe I are see you face on American ad-ver-tise-ment. I are hear you are very grade man ad these America," said the child of Stephen Wainwright.

He winced, and yet grew warm with pride and longing at the girl's delicious accent. He, too, tried to smile back at her, but something sharp bit at the man's eyelids.

"No, Sunny. Try and think. Throw your mind far back—back to your sixth year, if that may be."

Sunny's eyes, resting now in troubled question upon the face before her, grew slowly fixed and enlarged. Through the fogs of memory slowly, like a vision of the past, she seemed to see again a little child in a fragrant garden. She was standing by the rim of a pool, and the man opposite her now was at her side. He was dressed in Japanese kimona and hakama, and Sunny remembered that then he was always laughing at her, shaking the flower weighted trees above her, till the petals fell in a white and pink shower upon her little head and shoulders. She was stretching out her hands, catching the falling blossoms, and, delightedly exclaiming that the flying petals were tiny birds fluttering through the air. She was leaning over the edge of the pool, blowing the petals along the water, playing with her father that they were white prayer ships, carrying the petitions to the gods who waited on the other side. She remembered drowsing against the arm of the man; of being tossed aloft, her face cuddled against his neck; of passing under the great wistaria arbour. Ah, yes! how clearly she recalled it now! As her father transferred her to her mother's arms, he bent and drew that mother into his embrace also.

Two great tears welled up in the eyes of Sunny, but ere they could fall, the distance between her and her father had vanished. Stephen Wainwright, kneeling on the floor by his long-lost child, had drawn her hungrily into his arms.

"My own little girl!" said "The Man of Steel."

CHAPTER XVIII

Stephen Wainwright, holding his daughter jealously in his arms, felt those long-locked founts of emotion that had been pent up behind his steely exterior bursting all bounds. He had the immense feeling that he wanted for evermore to cherish and guard this precious thing that was all his own.

"Our actions are followed by their consequences as surely as a body by its shadow," says the Japanese proverb, and that cruel act of his mad youth had haunted the days of this man, who had achieved all that some men sell their souls for in life. And yet the greatest of all prizes had escaped him—peace of mind. Even now, as he held Sunny in his arms, he was consumed by remorse and anguish.

In his crowded life of fortune and fame, and a social career at the side of the brilliant woman who bore his name, Stephen Wainwright's best efforts had been unavailing to obliterate from his memory that tragic face that like a flower petal on a stream he had so lightly blown away. O-Haru-no was her name then, and she was the child of a Japanese woman of caste, whose marriage to an attaché of a Russian embassy had, in its time, created a furore in the capital. Her father had perished in a shipwreck at sea, and her mother had returned to her people, there, in her turn, to perish from grief and the cold neglect of the Japanese relatives who considered her marriage a blot upon the family escutcheon.

Always a lover and collector of beautiful things, Wainwright had harkened to the enthusiastic flights of a friend, who had "discovered" an incomparable piece of Satsuma, and had accompanied him to an old mansion, once part of a Satsuma yashiki, there to find that his friend's "piece of Satsuma" was a living work of art, a little piece of bric-a-brac that the collector craved to add to his collections. He had purchased O-Haru-no for a mere song, for her white skin had been a constant reproach and shame in the house of her ancestors. Moreover, this branch of the ancient family had fallen upon meagre days, and despite their pride, they were not above bartering this humble descendant for the gold of the American. O-Haru-no escaped with joy from the harsh atmosphere of the house of her ancestors to the gay home of her purchaser.

The fact that he had practically bought his wife, and that she had been willing to become a thing of barter and sale, had from the first caused the man to regard her lightly. We value things often, not by their intrinsic value, but by the price we have paid for them, and O-Haru-no had been thrown upon the bargain counter of life. However, it was not in Stephen Wainwright's nature to resist anything as pretty as the wife he had bought. A favourite and sardonic jest of his at that time was that she was the choicest piece in his collections, and that some day he purposed to put her in a glass case, and present her to the Museum of Art of his native city. Had indeed Stephen Wainwright seen the dancer, as she lay among her brilliant robes, her wide sleeves outspread like the wings of a butterfly, and that perfectly chiselled face on which the smile that had made her famous still seemed faintly to linger, he might have recalled that utterance of the past, and realised that no object of art in the great museum of which his people were so proud, could compare with this masterpiece of Death's grim hand.

He tried to delude himself with the thought that the temporary wife of his young days was but an incident, part of an idyll that had no place in the life of the man of steel, who had seized upon life with strong, hot hands.

But Sunny! His own flesh and blood, the child whose hair had suggested her name. Despite the galloping years she persisted ever in his memory. He thought of her constantly, of her strange little ways, her pretty coaxing ways, her smile, her charming love of the little live things, her perception of beauty, her closeness to nature. There was a quality of psychic sweetness about her, something rare and delicate that appealed to the epicure as exquisite and above all price. It was not his gold that had purchased Sunny. She was a gift of the gods and his memory of his child contained no flaw.

It was part of his punishment that the woman he married after his return to America from Japan should have drifted farther and farther apart from him with the years. Intuitively, his wife had recognised that hungry heart behind the man's cold exterior. She knew that the greatest urge in the character of this man was his desire for children. From year to year she suffered the agony of seeing the frustration of their hopes. Highstrung and imaginative, Mrs. Wainwright feared that her husband would acquire a dislike for her. The idea persisted like a monomania. She sought distraction from this ghost that arose between them in social activities and passionate work in the cause of woman's suffrage. It was her husband's misfortune that his nature was of that unapproachable sort that seldom lets down the mask, a man who retired within himself, and sought resources of comfort where indeed they were not to be found. Grimly, cynically, he watched the devastating effects of their separated interests, and in time she, too, in a measure was cast aside, in thought at least, just as the first wife had been. Stephen Wainwright grew grimmer and colder with the years, and the name applied to him was curiously suitable.

This was the man whose tears were falling on the soft hair of the strange girl from Japan. He had lifted her hat, that he might again see that hair, so bright and pretty that had first suggested her name. With awkward gentleness, he smoothed it back from the girl's thin little face.

"Sunny, you know your father now, fully, don't you? Tell me that you do—that you have not forgotten me. You were within a few weeks of six when I went away, and we were the greatest of pals. Surely you have not forgotten altogether. It seems just the other day you were looking at me, just as you are now. It does not seem to me as if you have changed at all. You are still my little girl. Tell me—you have not forgotten your father altogether, have you?"

"No. Those year they are push away. You are my Chichi (papa). I so happy see you face again."

She held him back, her two hands on his shoulders, and now, true to her sex, she prepared to demand a favour from her father.

"Now I think you are going to give Katy and me mos' bes' job ad you business."

"Job? Who is Katy?"

"I are not told you yet of Katy. Katy are my frien'."

"You've told me nothing. I must know everything that has happened to you since I left Japan."

"Thas too long ago," said Sunny sadly, "and I am hongry. I lig' eat liddle bit something."

"What! You've had no lunch?"

She told him the incident of the dog meat, not stopping to explain just then who Katy was, and how she had come to be with her. He leaned over to the desk and pushed the button. Miss Holliwell, coming to the door, saw a sight that for the first time in her years of service with Senator Wainwright took away her composure. Her employer was kneeling by a chair on which was seated the strange girl. Her hat was off, and she was holding one of his hands with both of hers. Even then he did not break the custom of years and explain or confide in his secretary, and she saw to her amazement that the eyes of the man she secretly termed "the sphinx" were red. All he said was:

"Order a luncheon, Miss Holliwell. Have it brought up here. Have Mouquin rush it through. That is all."

Miss Holliwell slowly closed the door, but her amazement at what she had seen within was turned to indignation at what she encountered without. As the door opened, Katy pressed up against the keyhole, fell back upon the floor. During the period when Sunny had been in the private office of Miss Holliwell's employer, she had had her hands full with the curious young person left behind. Katy had found relief from her pent-up curiosity in an endless stream of questions and gratuitous remarks which she poured out upon the exasperated secretary. Katy's tongue and spirit were entirely undaunted by the chilling monosyllabic replies of Miss Holliwell, and the latter was finally driven to the extremity of requesting her to wait in the outer office:

"I'm awfully busy," said the secretary, "and really when you chatter like that I cannot concentrate upon my work."

To which, with a wide friendly smile, rejoined Katy:

"Cheer up, Miss Frozen-Face. Mums the word from this time on."

"Mum" she actually kept, but her alert pose, her cocked-up ears and eyes, glued upon the door had such a quality of upset about them that Miss Holliwell found it almost as difficult to concentrate as when her tongue had rattled along. Now here she was engaged in the degrading employment of listening and seeing what was never intended for her ears and eyes. Miss Holliwell pushed her indignantly away.

"What do you *mean* by doing a thing like that?"

Between what she had seen inside her employer's private office, and the actions of this young gamin, Miss Holliwell was very much disturbed. She betook herself to the seat with a complete absence of her cultivated composure. When Katy said, however:

"Gee! I wisht I knew whether Sunny is safe in there with that gink," Miss Holliwell was forced to raise her hand to hide a smile that would come despite her best efforts. For once in her life she gave the wrong number, and was cross with the girl at the telephone desk because it was some time before Mouquin's was reached. The carefully ordered meal dictated by Miss Holliwell aroused in the listening Katy such mixed emotions, that, as the secretary hung up the receiver, the hungry youngster leaned over and said in a hoarse pleading whisper:

"Say, if you're orderin' for Sunny, make it a double."

Inside, Sunny was telling her father her story. "Begin from the first," he had said. "Omit nothing. I must know everything about you."

Graphically, as they waited for the lunch, she sketched in all the sordid details of her early life, the days of their mendicancy making the man feel immeasurably mean. Sitting at the desk now, his eyes shaded with his hand, he gritted his teeth, and struck the table with repeated soundless blows when his daughter told him of Hirata. But something, a feeling more penetrating than pain, stung Stephen Wainwright when she told him of those warmhearted men who had come into her life like a miracle and taken the place that he should have been there to fill. For the first time he interrupted her to take down the names of her friends, one by one, on a pad of paper. Professor Barrowes, Zoologist and Professor of Archeology. Wainwright had heard of him somewhere recently. Yes, he recalled him now. Some dispute about a recent "find" of the Professor's. A question raised as to the authenticity of the fossil. Opposition to its being placed in the Museum—Newspaper discussion. An effort on the Professor's part to raise funds for further exploration in Canada northwest.

Robert Mapson, Jr. Senator Wainwright knew the reporter slightly. He had covered stories in which Senator Wainwright was interested. On the *Comet*. Sunny's father knew the *Comet* people well.

Lamont Potter, Jr. Philadelphia people. His firm did business with them. Young Potter at Bellevue.

J. Lyon Crawford, son of a man once at college with Wainwright. Sunny's father recalled some chaffing joke at the club anent "Jinx's" political ambitions. As a prospect in politics he had seemed a joke to his friends.

And, last, J. Addison Hammond, Jr., "Jerry."

How Sunny had pronounced that name! There was that about that soft inflection that caused her father to hold his pencil suspended, while a stab of jealousy struck him.

"What does he do, Sunny?"

"Ho! He are goin' be grade artist-arki-tuck. He make so beautiful pictures, and he have mos' beautiful thought on inside his head. He goin' to make all these city loog beautiful. He show how make 'partment houses, where all god light and there's garden grow on top, and there's house where they not put out liddle bebby on street. He's go sleep and play on those garden on top house."

Her father, his elbow on desk, his chin cupped on his hand, watched the girl's kindling face, and suffered pangs that he could not analyse. Quietly he urged her to continue her story. Unwilling she turned from

Jerry, but came back always to him. Of her life in Jerry's apartment, of Hatton and his "yuman 'ankerings"; of Itchy, with his two fleas; of Mr. and Mrs. Satsuma in the gold cage, of Count and Countess Taguchi who swam in the glass bowl; of the honourable mice; of the butcher and janitor gentlemen; of Monty, of Bobs, of Jinx, who had asked her to marry them, and up to the day when Mrs. Hammond and Miss Falconer had come to the apartment and turned her out. Then a pause to catch her breath in a wrathful sob, to continue the wistful tale of her prayer to Kuonnon in the raging, noisy street; of the mother's gentle spirit that had gone with her on the dark long road that lead to—Katy.

It was then that Miss Holliwell tapped, and the waiters came in with the great loaded trays held aloft, bearing the carefully ordered meal and the paraphernalia that accompanies a luncheon de luxe. Someone besides the waiters had slipped by Miss Holliwell. Katy, clucking with her tongue against the roof of her mouth, tried to attract the attention of Sunny, whose back was turned. Sniffing those delicious odours, Katy came farther into the room, and following the clucking she let out an unmistakably false cough and loud Ahem!

This time, Sunny turned, saw her friend, and jumped up from her seat and ran to her. Said Katy in a whisper:

"Gee! You're smarter than I gave you credit for being. Got him going, ain't you? Well, pull his leg while the going's good, and say, Sunny, if them things on the tray are for you, remember, I gave you half my hot dogs and I always say——"

"This are my frien', Katy," said Sunny proudly, as the very grave faced man whom Katy had tried to trip came forward and took Katy's hand in a tight clasp.

"Katy, this are my—Chichi—Mr. Papa," said Sunny.

Katy gasped, staring with wide open mouth from Senator Wainwright to Sunny. Her head reeled with the most extravagantly romantic tale that instantly flooded it. Then with a whoop curiously like that of some small boy, Katy grasped hold of Sunny about the waist.

"Whuroo!" cried Katy. "I *knew* you was a princess. Gee. It's just like a dime novel—better than any story in Hoist's even."

There in the dignified office of the steel magnate the girl from the east side drew his daughter into one of the most delicious shimmies, full of sheer fun and impudent youth. For the first time in years, Senator Wainwright threw back his head and burst into laughter.

Now these two young radiant creatures, who could dance while they hungered, were seated before that gorgeous luncheon. Sunny's father lifted the top from the great planked steak, entirely surrounded on the board with laced browned potatoes, ornamental bits of peas, beans, lima and string, asparagus, cauliflower and mushrooms.

Sunny let forth one long ecstatic sigh as she clasped her hands together, while Katy laid both hands piously upon her stomach and raising her eyes as if about to deliver a solemn Grace, she said:

"Home, sweet home, was never like this!"

CHAPTER XIX

Society enjoys a shock. It craves sensation. When that brilliant and autocratic leader returned from several months' absence abroad, with a young daughter, of whose existence no one had ever heard, her friends were mystified. When, with the most evident pride and fondness she referred to the fact that her daughter had spent most of her life in foreign lands, and was the daughter of Senator Wainwright's first wife, speculation was rife. That the Senator had been previously married, that he had a daughter of eighteen years, set all society agog, and expectant to see the girl, whose debut was to be made at a large coming out party given by her mother in her honour. The final touch of mystery and romance was added by the daughter herself. An enterprising society reporter, had through the magic medium of a card from her chief, Mr. Mapson, of the New York *Comet*, obtained a special interview with Miss Wainwright on the eve of her ball, and the latter had confided to the incredulous and delighted newspaper woman the fact that she expected to be married at an early date. The announcement, however, lost some of its thrill when Miss Wainwright omitted the name of the happy man. Application to her mother brought forth the fact that that personage knew no more about this coming event than the "throb sister," as she called herself. Mrs. Wainwright promptly denied the story, pronouncing it a probable prank of Miss Sunny and her friend, Miss Clarry. Here Mrs. Wainwright sighed. She always sighed at the mention of Katy's name, sighed indulgently, yet hopelessly. The latter had long since been turned over to the efficient hands of a Miss Woodhouse, a lady from Bryn Mawr, who had accompanied the Wainwright party abroad. Her especial duty in life was to refine Katy, a task not devoid of entertainment to said competent young person from Bryn Mawr, since it stirred to literary activity certain slumbering talents, and in due time Katy, through the pen of Miss Woodhouse, was firmly pinned on paper.

However, this is not Katy's story, though it may not be inapropos to mention here that the Mrs. J. Lyon Crawford, Jr., who for so long queened it over, bossed, bullied and shepherded the society of New York, was under the skin ever the same little General who had marched forth with her army of one down the steps of that east side tenement house, with hat pin ostentatiously and dangerously apparent to the craven rat of the east side.

Coming back to Sunny. The newspaper woman persisting that the story had been told her with utmost candour and seriousness, Mrs. Wainwright sent for her daughter. Sunny, questioned by her mother, smilingly confirmed the story.

"But, my dear," said Mrs. Wainwright, "You know no young men yet. Surely you are just playing. It's a game between you and Katy, isn't it, dear? Katy is putting you up to it, I'm sure."

"No, mama, Katy are—is—not do so. *I* am! It is true! I am going to make marriage wiz American gentleman mebbe very soon."

"Darling, I believe I'd run along. That will do for just now, dear. *I'll* speak to Miss Ah—what is the name?"

"Holman, of the *Comet*."

"Ah, yes, Miss Holman. Run along, dear," in a tone an indulgent mother uses to a baby. Then with her club smile turned affably on Miss Holman: "Our little Sunny is so mischievous. Now I'm quite sure she and Miss Clarry are playing some naughty little game. I don't believe I'd publish that if I were you, Miss Holman."

Miss Holman laughed in Mrs. Wainwright's face, which brought the colour to a face that for the last few months had radiated such good humour upon the world. Mrs. Wainwright smiled, now discomfited, for she knew that the newspaper woman not only intended to print Sunny's statement, but her mother's denial.

"Now, Miss Holman, your story will have no value, in view of the fact that the name of the man is not mentioned."

"I thought that a defect at first," said Miss Holman, shamelessly, "but I'm inclined to think it will add to the interest. Our readers dote on mysteries, and I'll cover the story on those lines. Later I'll do a bit of sleuthing on the man end. We'll get him," and the man-like young woman nodded her head briskly and betook herself from the Wainwright residence well satisfied with her day's work.

An appeal to the editor of the *Comet* on the telephone brought back the surprising answer that they would not print the story if Sunny—that editor referred to the child of Senator Wainwright as "Sunny"—herself denied it. He requested that "Sunny" be put on the wire. Mrs. Wainwright was especially indignant over this, because she knew that that editor had arisen to his present position entirely through a certain private "pull" of Senator Wainwright. Of course, the editor himself did not know this, but Senator Wainwright's wife did, and she thought him exceedingly unappreciative and exasperating.

Mrs. Wainwright sought Sunny in her room. Here she found that bewildering young person with her extraordinary friend enthusing over a fashion book devoted to trousseaux and bridal gowns. They looked up with flushed faces, and Mrs. Wainwright could not resist a feeling of resentment at the thought that her daughter (she never thought of Sunny as "stepdaughter") should give her confidence to Miss Clarry in preference to her. However, she masked her feelings, as only Mrs. Wainwright could, and with a smile to Katy advised her that Miss Woodhouse was waiting for her. Katy's reply, "Yes, ma'am—I mean, Aunt Emma," was submissive and meek enough, but it was hard for Mrs. Wainwright to overlook that very pronounced wink with which Katy favoured Sunny ere she departed.

"And now, dear," said Mrs. Wainwright, putting her arm around Sunny, "tell me all about it."

Sunny, who loved her dearly, cuddled against her like a child, but nevertheless shook her bright head.

"Ho! That is secret I not tell. I are a tomb."

"Tomb?"

"Yes, thas word lig' Katy use when she have secret. She say it are—is—lock up in tomb."

"To think," said Mrs. Wainwright jealously, "that you prefer to confide in a stranger like Katy rather than your mother."

"No, I not told Katy yet," said Sunny quickly. "She have ask me one tousan' time, and I are not tol' her."

"But, darling, surely you want *me* to know. Is he any young man we are acquainted with?"

Sunny, finger thoughtfully on her lip, considered.

"No-o, I think you are not know him yet."

"Is he one of the young men who—er——"

It was painful for Mrs. Wainwright to contemplate that chapter in Sunny's past when she had been the ward of four strange young men. In fact, she had taken Sunny abroad immediately after that remarkable time when her husband had brought the strange young girl to the house and for the first time she had learned of Sunny's existence. Life had taken on a new meaning to Mrs. Wainwright after that. Suddenly she comprehended the meaning of having someone to live for. Her life and work had a definite purpose and impetus. Her husband's child had closed the gulf that had yawned so long between man and wife, and was threatening to separate them forever. Her love for Sunny, and her pride in the girl's beauty and charm was almost pathetic. Had she been the girl's own mother, she could not have been more indulgent or anxious for her welfare.

Sunny, not answering the last question, Mrs. Wainwright went over in her mind each one of the young men whose ward Sunny had been. The first three, Jinx, Monty and Bobs, she soon rejected as possibilities. There remained Jerry Hammond. Private inquiries concerning Jerry had long since established the fact that he had been for a number of years engaged to a Miss Falconer. Mrs. Wainwright had been much distressed because Sunny insisted on writing numerous letters to Jerry while abroad. It seemed very improper, so she told the girl, to write letters to another woman's fiancé. Sunny agreed with this most earnestly, and after a score of letters had gone unanswered she promised to desist.

Mrs. Wainwright appreciated all that Mr. Hammond had done for her daughter. Sunny's father had indeed expressed that appreciation in that letter (a similar one had been sent to all members of the Sunny Syndicate) penned immediately after he had found Sunny. He had, moreover, done everything in his power privately to advance the careers and interests of the various men who had befriended his daughter. But for his engagement to Miss Falconer, Mrs. Wainwright would not have had the slightest objection to Sunny continuing her friendship with this Mr. Hammond, but really it was hardly the proper thing under the circumstances. However, she was both peeved and relieved when Sunny's many epistles remained unanswered for months, and then a single short letter that was hardly calculated to revive Sunny's childish passion for this Jerry arrived. Jerry wrote:

"Dear Sunny.

Glad get your many notes. Have been away. Glad you are happy. Hope see you when you return.

JERRY."

A telegram would have contained more words, the ruffled Mrs. Wainwright was assured, and she acquired a prejudice against Jerry, despite all the good she had heard of him. From that time on her rôle was to, as far as lay in her power, distract the dear child from thought of the man who very evidently cared nothing about her.

Of course, Mrs. Wainwright did not know of that illness of Jerry Hammond when he had hovered between life and death. She did not know that all of Sunny's letters had come to his hand at one time, unwillingly given up by Professor Barrowes, who feared a relapse from the resulting excitement. She did not know that that shaky scrawl was due to the fact that Jerry was sitting up in bed, and had penned twenty or more letters to Sunny, in which he had exhausted all of the sweet words of a lover's vocabulary, and then had stopped short to contemplate the fact that he had done absolutely nothing in the world to prove himself worthy of Sunny, had torn up the aforementioned letters, and penned the blank scrawl that told the daughter of Senator Wainwright nothing.

But it was shortly after that that Jerry began to "come back." He started upon the highroad to health, and his recuperation was so swift that he was able to laugh at the protesting and anxious Barrowes, who moved heaven and earth to prevent the young man from returning to his work. Jerry had been however, "away" long enough, so he said, and he fell upon his work with such zeal that no mere friend or mother could stop him. Never had that star of Beauty, of which he had always dreamed, seemed so close to Jerry as now. Never had the incentive to succeed been so vital and gloriously necessary. At the end of all his efforts, he saw no longer the elusive face of the imaginary "Beauty," of which he loved to tell Sunny, and which he despaired ever to reach. What was a figment of the imagination now took a definite lovely form. At the end of his rainbow was the living face of Sunny.

And so with a song within his heart, a light in his eyes, and a spring to his step, with kind words for everyone he met, Jerry Hammond worked and waited.

Mrs. Wainwright, by this time, knew the futility of trying to force Sunny to reveal her secret. Not only was she very Japanese in her ability to keep a secret when she chose, but she was Stephen Wainwright's child. Her mother knew that for months she had neither seen nor written to Jerry Hammond, for Sunny herself had told her so, when questioned. Who then was the mysterious fiancé? Could it possibly be someone she had known in Japan? This thought caused Mrs. Wainwright considerable trepidation. She feared the possibility of a young Russian, a Japanese, a missionary. To make sure that Jerry was not the one Sunny had in mind, she asked the girl whether he had ever proposed to her, and Sunny replied at once, very sadly:

"No-o. I ask him do so, but he do not do so. He are got 'nother girl he marry then. Jinx and Monty and Bobs are all ask me marry wiz them, but Jerry never ask so."

"Oh, my dear, did you really *ask* him to ask you to marry him?"

"Ho! I hint for him do so," said Sunny, "but he do not do so. Thas very sad for me," she admitted dejectedly.

"Very fortunate, I call it," said Mrs. Wainwright.

Thus Jerry's elimination was completed, and for the nonce the matter of Sunny's marriage was dropped pro tem, to be revived, however, on the night of her ball, when the story appeared under leaded type in the *Comet*.

CHAPTER XX

There have been many marvellous balls given in the City of New York, but none exceeding the famous Cherry Blossom ball. The guests stepped into a vast ball room that had been transformed into a Japanese garden in spring. On all sides, against the walls, and made into arbours and groves, cherry trees in full blossom were banked, while above and over the galleries dripped the long purple and white heads of the wistaria. The entire arch of the ceiling was covered with cherry branches, and the floor was of heavy glass, in imitation of a lake in which the blossoms were reflected.

Through a lane of slender bamboo the guests passed to meet, under a cherry blossom bower, the loveliest bud of the season, Sunny, in a fairy-like maline and chiffon frock, springing out about her diaphanously, and of the pale pink and white colors of the cherry blossoms. Sunny, with her bright, shining hair coifed by the hand of an artist; Sunny, with her first string of perfect pearls and a monstrous feather fan, that when dropped seemed to cover half her short fluffy skirts. Sunny, with the brightest eyes, darting in and out and looking over the heads of her besieging guests, laughing, nodding, breathlessly parrying the questions that poured in on all sides. Everybody wanted to know who *the* man was.

"Oh, do tell us who he is," they would urge, and Sunny would shake her bright head, slowly unfurl her monstrous fan, and with it thoughtfully at her lips she would say:

"Ho yes, it are true, and mebbe I will tell you some nother day."

Now among those present at Sunny's party were five men whose acquaintance the readers of this story have already made. It so happened that they were very late in arriving at the Wainwright dance, this being due to the fact that one of their number had to be brought there by physical force. Jerry, at dinner, had read that story in the *Comet*, and was reduced to such a condition of distraction that it was only by the united efforts of his four friends that he was forcibly shoved into that car. The party arrived late, as stated, and it may be recorded that as Sunny's eyes searched that sea of faces before her, moving to the music of the orchestra and the tinkle of the Japanese bells, they lost somewhat of their shining look, and became so wistful that her father, sensitive to every change in the girl, never left her side; but he could not induce the girl to dance. She remained with her parents in the receiving arbor. Suddenly two spots of bright rose came to the cheeks of Sunny, and she arose on tip-toes, just as she had done as a child on the tight rope. She saw that arriving party approaching, and heard Katy's voice as she husbanded them to what she called "the royal throne."

At this juncture, and when he was within but a few feet of the "throne" Jerry saw Sunny. One long look passed between them, and then, shameless to relate, Jerry ducked into that throng of dancers. To further escape the wrathful hands of his friends, he seized some fat lady hurriedly about the waist and dragged her upon the glass floor. His rudeness covered up with as much tact as his friends could muster, they proceeded, as far as lay in their power, to compensate for his defection. They felt no sympathy nor patience with the acts of Jerry. Were they not all in the same boat, and equally stung by the story of Sunny's engagement?

Both hands held out, Sunny welcomed her friends. First Professor Barrowes:

"Ho! How it is good ad my eyes see your kind face again."

Alas! for Sunny's several months with especial tutors and governesses, and the beautiful example of Mrs. Wainwright. Always in moments of excitement she lapsed into her strangely-twisted English speech and topsy-turvy grammar.

Professor Barrowes, with the dust in his eyes and brain of that recent triumphant trip into the northwest of Canada, brushed aside by the illness of his friend, was on solid enough earth as Sunny all but hugged him. Bowing, beaming, chuckling, he took the fragrant little hand in his own, and with the pride and glow of a true discoverer, his eye scanned the fairylike creature before him.

"Ah! Miss—ah—Sunny. The pleasure is mine—entirely mine, I assure you. May I add that you still, to me, strongly resemble the child who came upon the tight rope, with a smile upon her face, and a dewdrop on her cheek.

"May I add," continued Professor Barrowes, "that it is my devout hope, my dear, that you will always remain unchanged? I hope so devoutly. I wish it."

"Ho! Mr. dear Professor, I am jos' nothing but little moth. Nothing moach good on these earth. But you—you are do so moach I am hear. You tich all those worl' *how* those worl' are be ad the firs' day of all! Tell me 'bout what happen to you. Daikoku (God of Fortune) he have been kind to you—yes?"

"Astounding kind—amazingly so. There is much to tell. If you will allow me, at an early date, I will do myself the pleasure of calling upon you, and—ah—going into detail. I believe you will be much interested in recent discoveries in a hitherto unexplored region of the Canadian northwest, where I am convinced the largest number of fossils of the post pliocene and quaternary period are to be found. I had the pleasure of assisting in bringing back to the United States the full-sized skeleton of a dinornis. You no doubt have heard of the aspersions regarding its authenticity, but I believe we have made our—er—opponents appear pretty small, thanks to the aid of your father and other friends. In point of fact, I may say, I am indebted to your father for an undeserved recommendation, and a liberal donation, which will make possible the fullest research, and establish beyond question the—ah——"

Miss Holliwell, smiling and most efficiently and inconspicuously managing the occasion, noting the congestion about Sunny, and the undisguised expressions of deepening disgust and impatience on the faces of Sunny's other friends, here interposed. She slipped her hand through the Professor's arm, and with a murmured:

"Oh, Professor Barrowes, do try this waltz with me. It's one of the old ones, and this is Leap Year, so I am going to ask you."

Now Miss Holliwell had had charge of all the matters pertaining to the dinornis; her association with Professor Barrowes had been both pleasant and gratifying to the man of science.

If anyone imagines that sixty-year-old legs cannot move with the expedition and grace of youth, he should have witnessed the gyrations and motions of the legs of Professor Barrowes as he guided the Senator's secretary through the mazes of the waltz.

Came then Monty, upright and rosy, and as shamelessly young as when over four years before, at seventeen, he imagined himself wise and aged-looking with his bone-ribbed glasses. The down was still on Monty's cheek, and the adoration of the puppy still in his eyes.

"Sunny! It does my soul good to see you. You look perfectly great—yum-yum. Jove, you gave us a fright, all right. Haven't got over it yet. Looked for you in the morgue, Sunny, and here you are shining like—like a star."

"Monty! That face of you will make me always shine like star. What you are doing these day?"

"Oh, just a few little things. Nothing to mention," returned Monty, with elaborate carelessness, his heart thumping with pride and yearning to pour out the full tale into the sympathetic pink ear of Sunny. "I got a year or two still to put in—going up to Johns Hopkins; then, Sunny, I've a great job for next summer—between the postgraduate work. I'll get great, practical training from a field that—well——I'm going to Panama, Sunny. Connection with fever and sanitary work. Greatest opportunity of lifetime. I'm to be first assistant—it's the literal truth, to——" He whispered a name in Sunny's ear which caused her to start back, gasping with admiration.

"Monty; how I am proud of you!"

"Oh, it's nothing much. Don't know why in the world they picked *me*. My work wasn't better than the other chaps. I was conscientious enough and interested of course, but so were the other fellows. You could have knocked me down with a feather when they picked me for the job. Why, I was fairly stunned by the news. Haven't got over it yet. Your father knows Dr. Roper, the chief, you know. Isn't the world small? Say, Sunny, whose the duck you're engaged to? G'wan, tell your old chum."

"Ho, Monty, I will tell you—tonide mebbe some time."

"Here, here, Monty, you've hogged enough of Sunny's attention. My turn now." Bobs pushed the unwilling Monty along, and the youngster, pretending a lofty indifference to the challenging smiles directed at him by certain members of the younger set, was nevertheless soon slipping over the floor, with the prettiest one of them all, whom Mrs. Wainwright especially led him to.

Bobs meanwhile was grinning at Sunny, while she, with a maternal eye, examined "dear Bobs," and noted that he had gotten into his clothes hastily, but that nevertheless he was the same charming friend.

"By gum, you look positively edible," was his greeting. "What you been doing with yourself, and what's this latest story I'm hearing about your marrying some Sonofagun?"

"Bobs, I are goin' to tell you 'bout those Sonofagun some time this nide," smiled Sunny, "but I want to know firs' of all tings, what you are do, dear Bobs?"

"I?" Bobs rose up and down on his polished toes. "City editor of the *Comet*, old top, that's my job. Youngest ever known on the desk, but not, I hope, the least competent."

"Ho, Bobs. You *are* one whole editor man! How I am proud of you. Now you are goin' right up to top notch. Mebbe by'n by you get to be ambassador ad udder country and——"

"Whew-w! How can a mere man climb to the heights you expect of him. What I want to know is—how about that marriage story? I printed it, because it was good stuff, but who is the lucky dog? Come on, now, you know you can tell me anything."

"Ho, Bobs, I *are* goin' tell you anything. Loog, Bobs, here are a frien' I wan' you speag ad. She also have wrote a book. Her name are—is Miss Woodenhouse. She is ticher to my frien', Miss Clarry. She are———"

"Are! Sunny?"

"'Am'. She am—no, is, very good ticher. She am—is—make me and Katy spik and ride English jos same English lady."

The young and edified instructor of Katy Clarry surveyed the young and edified editor of the New York *Comet* with a quizzical eye. The young editor in question returned that quizzical glance, grinned, offered his arm, and they whirled off to the music of a rippling two-step.

Sunny had swung around and seized the two plump soft hands of Jinx, at whose elbow Katy was pressing. Katy, much to her delight, had been assisting Miss Holliwell in caring for the arriving guests, and had indeed quite surprised and amused that person by her talent for organisation and real ability. Katy was in her element as she bustled about, in somewhat the proprietary manner of the floor walkers and the lady heads of departments in the stores where Katy had one time worked.

"Jinx, Jinx, Jinx! My eyes are healty jos' loog ad you! I am *thad* glad see you speag also wiz my bes' frien', Katy." She clapped her hands excitedly. "How I thing it nize that you and Katy be———"

Katy coughed loudly. Sunny's ignorance at times was extremely distressing. Katy had a real sympathy for Mrs. Wainwright at certain times. Jinx had blushed as red as a peony.

"Have a heart, Sunny!"

Nevertheless he felt a sleepish pride in the thought that Sunny's best friend should have singled him out for special attention. Jinx, though the desired one of aspiring mothers, was not so popular with the maidens, who were pushed forward and adjured to regard him as a most desirable husband. Katy was partial to flesh. She had no patience with the artist who declared that bones were æsthetic and to suit his taste he liked to hear the bones rattle. Katy averred that there was something awfully cosy about fat people.

"I hear some grade news of you, Jinx," said Sunny admiringly. "I hear you are got nomin—ation be on staff those governor."

"That's only the beginning, Sunny. I'm going in for politics a bit. Life too purposeless heretofore, and the machine wants me. At least, I've been told so. Your father, Sunny, has been doggone nice about it—a real friend. You know there was a bunch of city hicks that thought it fun to laugh at the idea of a fat man holding down any public job, but I guess the fat fellow can put it over some of the other bunch."

"Ho! I should say that so."

"Look at President Taft," put in Katy warmly. "He weighs more'n you do, I'll bet."

"Give a fellow a chance," said Jinx bashfully. "If I keep on, I'll soon catch up with him."

"Sunny," said Katy in her ear, "I feel like Itchy. You remember you told me how after a bath he liked to roll himself in the dirt because he missed his fleas. That's me all over. I miss my fleas. I ain—aren't used to being refined. Gee! I hope Miss Woodhouse didn't hear me say that. If she catches me talking like that—good-night! D'she ever make *you* feel like a two-spot?"—Scorch with a *look*! Good-night!"

A broad grin lighted up Katy's wide Irish face. Shoving her arm recklessly through Jinx's, she said:

"Come along, old skate, let's show 'em on the floor what reglar dancers like you and me can do."

Sunny watched them with shining eyes, and once as they whirled by, Katy's voice floated above the murmurs of the dance and music:

"Gee! How light you are on your feet! Plump men usually are. I always say———"

And Katy and Jinx, Monty and Bobs and the Professor and all her friends were lost to view in that moving, glittering throng of dancers, upon whom, like fluttering moths the cherry blossom petals were dropping from above alighting upon their heads and shoulders and giving them that festival look that Sunny knew so well in Japan. She had a breathing space for a spell, and now that very wistful longing look stole like a shadow back to the girl's young face. All unconsciously a sigh escaped her. Instantly her father was at her side.

"You want something, my darling?"

"Yes, papa. You love me very much, papa?"

"*Do* I? If there's anything in the world you want that I can give you, you have only to ask, my little girl."

"Then papa, you see over dere that young man stand. You see him?"

"Young Hammond?"

"Jerry." Her very pronouncement of his name was a caress. "Papa, I wan speag to him. All these night I have wan see him. See, wiz my fan I are do lig' this, and nod my head, and wiz my finger, too, I call him, but he do not come," dejectedly. "Loog! I will do so again. You see!" She made an unmistakable motion with her hand and fan at Jerry and that unhappy young fool turned his back and slunk behind some artificial camphor trees.

"By George!" said Senator Wainwright. "Sunny, do you want me to bring that young puppy to you?"

"Papa, Jerry are not a puppy, but jus' same, I wan' you bring him unto me. Please. And then, when he come, please you and mamma stand liddle bit off, and doan let nobody else speag ad me. I are got something I wan ask Jerry all by me."

The music had stopped, but the clapping hands of the dancers were clamouring for a repetition of the crooning dance song that had just begun its raging career in the metropolis. Sunny saw her father clap Jerry upon the shoulder. She saw his effort to escape, and her father's smiling insistence. A short interval of breathless suspense, and then the reluctant, very white, very stern young Jerry was standing before Sunny. He tried to avoid Sunny's glance, but, fascinated, found himself looking straight into the girl's eyes. She was smiling, but there was something in her dewy glance that reached out and twisted the boy's heart strings sadly.

"Jerry!" said Sunny softly, her great fan touching her lips, and looking up at him with such a glance that all his best resolves to continue calm seemed threatened with panic. He said, with what he flattered was an imitation of composure:

"Lovely day—er—night. How are you?"

"I are so happy I are lig' those soap bubble. I goin' burst away."

"Yes, naturally you would be happy. Beautiful day—er—night, isn't it?"

He resolved to avoid all personal topics. He would shoot small talk at her, and she should not suspect the havoc that was raging within him.

"How are your mother?"

"Well, thank you."

"How are your frien', Miss Falconer?"

"Don't know, I'm sure."

"Hatton are tol' me all 'bout her," said Sunny.

"Hatton? He's gone. I don't know where?"

"He are officer at Salavation Army. He come to our house, and my father give him money for those poor people. Hatton are tell me all 'bout you. I are sawry you sick long time, Jerry. Thas very sad news for me."

Jerry, tongue-tied for the moment, knew not what to say or where to look. Sunny's dear glance was almost more than he could bear.

"Beautiful room this. Decoration———"

"Jerry, that are your beautiful picture you are made. I am remember it all. One time you draw those picture like these for me, and you say thas mos' nize picture for party ever. I think so."

Jerry was silent.

"Jerry, how you are do ad those worl'? Please tell me. I lig' to hear. Are you make grade big success? Are you found those Beauty thad you are loog for always?"

"Beauty!" he said furiously. "I told you often enough that it was an elusive jade, that no one could ever reach. And as for success. I suppose I've made good enough. I was offered a partnership—I can't take it. I'll———I'll have to get away. Sunny, for God's sake, answer me. Is it true you are going to be married?"

Slowly the girl bowed with great seriousness, yet somehow her soft eyes rested in caress upon the young man's tortured face.

"Jerry," said Sunny dreamily, "this are the Year of Leap, and I are lig' ask you liddle bit question."

Jerry neither heard nor understood the significance of the girlish words. His young face had blanched. All the joy of life seemed to have been extinguished. Yet one last passionate question burst from him.

"Who—is—he?"

Slowly Sunny raised that preposterous fan. She brought it to her face, so that its great expanse acted as a screen and cut her and Jerry off from the rest of the world. Her bright lovely gaze sank right into Jerry's, and Sunny answered softly:

"*You!*"

Now what followed would furnish a true student of psychology with the most irrefutable proof of the devastating effect upon a young man of the superior and civilised west of association with a heathen people. Even the unsophisticated eye of Sunny saw that primitive purpose leap up in the eye of Jerry Hammond, as, held in leash only a moment, he proposed then and there to seize the girl bodily in his arms. It was at that moment that her oriental guile came to the top. Sunny stepped back, put out her hand, moved it along the wall, behind the cherry petalled foliage, and then while Jerry's wild, ecstatic intention brought him ever nearer to her, Sunny found and pushed the button on the wall.

Instantly the room was plunged into darkness. A babble of murmuring sounds and exclamations; laughter, the sudden ceasing of the music, a soft pandemonium had broken loose, but in that blissful moment of complete darkness, oblivious to all the world, feeling and seeing only each other, Jerry and Sunny kissed.

THE END